A BODY ON
FITZGERALD'S
BLUFF

Seaview Cottages Cozy Mystery #1

Anna Celeste Burke

Books by USA Today and Wall Street Journal Bestselling Author, Anna Celeste Burke

A Dead Husband Jessica Huntington Desert Cities
Mystery #1
A Dead Sister Jessica Huntington Desert Cities Mystery #2
A Dead Daughter Jessica Huntington Desert Cities
Mystery #3
A Dead Mother Jessica Huntington Desert Cities
Mystery #4
A Dead Cousin Jessica Huntington Desert Cities
Mystery #5
A Dead Nephew Jessica Huntington Desert Cities
Mystery #6 [2019]
Love A Foot Above the Ground Prequel to the Jessica
Huntington Desert Cities Mystery Series

Cowabunga Christmas! Corsario Cove Cozy Mystery #1
Gnarly New Year Corsario Cove Cozy Mystery #2
Heinous Habits, Corsario Cove Cozy Mystery #3
Radical Regatta, Corsario Cove Cozy Mystery #4 [2019]

Murder at Catmmando Mountain Georgie Shaw Cozy
Mystery #1
Love Notes in the Key of Sea Georgie Shaw Cozy
Mystery #2
All Hallows' Eve Heist Georgie Shaw Cozy Mystery #3
A Merry Christmas Wedding Mystery Georgie Shaw Cozy
Mystery #4

Dedication

Here's to finding the courage to start over when life throws us a curve—no matter how old we are!

Table of Contents

Acknowledgements   ix
Cast of Characters   xi
1. A Body on the Bluff   1
2. What Body?   13
3. Home Sweet Home   27
4. Dinner and a Murder   38
5. Resident Sugar Daddy   52
6. The County Hoosegow   62
7. Money or Men?   72
8. Rivals 'Til the End?   85
9. Money *and* Men   94
10. Scarves, Scones, and Scripts   101
11. A Bad Boy Shopper?   111
12. A Man Named Boo   123
13. Blue Shue Bribery   131
14. All in the Family   140
15. Murder, Men, and Motives   155
16. The Blue Haven Bluejackets   170
17. The Man Who's *Not* on the Bridge   180
18. Domino's Game   187
19. Good as Gold   204
Recipes   219
About the Author   231

Acknowledgements

Thanks to Peggy Hyndman for hanging in there through several edits of this book. I'm grateful for her help as A Body on Fitzgerald's Bluff has made its way from the *Summer Snoops and Cozy Crimes* limited edition, multi-author box set to become a standalone book! Her support and enthusiasm for this first book in a new series has been a big boost.

Another big thank you for the readers who support and encourage me—especially my "ARC Angels" who read my books before they're published. I appreciate the feedback many provide while I'm writing as well as their cheerleading. Some have even granted me permission to name a character after them! In this book it's a long list:

Rosemary Pfeiffer
JoAn Varner
Judi Stephenson
Tara Brown
Andrea Stoeckel
Doward Wilson
Valerie Bargewell
Robyn Chappell
Karen Vaughan
Carmel Schneider
Peggy Clayton
Donna Wolz
Jeanine Carlson
Penny Wilfort
Vicki Hardman

Thank you!

Cast of Characters

Dear reader, if you'd prefer to be surprised as each character is introduced please skip this section!

GRAND OLD LADY DETECTIVES:

Miriam Webster, who lives in Hemingway Cottage, was a bookkeeper, is a talented baker, and her fur baby is a Dalmatian, named Domino. Domino discovered the body behind Fitzgerald's Bluff.

Penelope Parker lives in Brontë Cottage, is a member of the Seaview Cottages Walkers Club, and has a Jack Russell terrier, named Emily. Penelope prefers to be called Charly in honor of her favorite writer, Charlotte Brontë, and is a retired criminology professor.

Cornelia "Neely" Conrad lives in Christie Cottage and is a self-proclaimed night owl who loves to read. Neely is retired and was an actress, turned costume designer and makeup artist.

Marty Monroe lives in Fitzgerald Cottage and is a member of the Seaview Cottages Walkers Club. Before retiring, Marty spent decades working as a buyer for high-end department stores.

Midge Gaylord lives in Austen Cottage and is a member of the Seaview Cottages Walkers Club. Midge is an ex-Army trauma care nurse, with ties to the local medical community.

OTHER SEAVIEW COTTAGES RESIDENTS AND EMPLOYEES:

Alyssa and Alfred "Alf" Gardener, known as *The* Gardeners, live in [Beatrix] Potter Cottage.

Carl Rodgers lives in Steinbeck Cottage and is the former manager of a collection agency.

Edgar Humphrey lives in Twain Cottage, is very rich, and loves young, attractive women.

Greta Bishop lives in Garbo Cottage and is a Realtor and a Seaview Cottages HOA board member.

Howard Humphrey is Edgar's nephew and rents the old Sinclair Cottage on the beach.

JoAn Varner is the clubhouse manager for Seaview Cottages.

Joe Torrance, who lives in Chandler Cottage, is a retired auto dealership service manager and mechanic.

Peggy Clayton is a Seaview Cottages HOA board member.

Robyn Chappell rents Shakespeare Cottage.

Rosemary Pfeiffer is the receptionist for Seaview Cottages Community Clubhouse.

THE VICTIM:

Diana Durand is the murder victim who was found behind a bluff near the beach.

LAW ENFORCEMENT:

Darnell Devers is a Deputy Sheriff who all the locals have various pet names for due to his "do as little as possible attitude."

Henry "Hank" Miller is the personable and competent lead detective assigned to investigate the death of Diana Durand.

Karen Vaughan, a pleasant young woman with a no-nonsense demeanor, is a Crime Scene Investigator.

SECONDARY CHARACTERS:

Andrea "Andi" Stoeckel is a sales clerk at the Blue Moon Boutique.

Blue Haven Bluejackets Summer Camp attendees, Nathan and Brandon, are young brothers who have important clues about what happened on the beach.

Boo is the nickname for the victim's San Francisco business partner.

Carmel Schneider is Neely Conrad's undercover name.

Dave Winick is a Blue Haven executive who dreams of being the resort's CEO.

Donna Wolz is the retired manager at Blue Moon Boutique.

Doward Wilson is a truck stop cook.

Jeanine Carlson was one of the victim's coworkers at Blue Moon Boutique.

Judi Stephenson is a Blue Moon Boutique sales clerk.

Mark Hudson sells merchandise at Blue Haven Pro Shop and gives golf lessons.

Mike Evans worked in Guest Services at Blue Haven Resort.

Penney Wilfort was the victim's immediate supervisor at the Blue Moon Boutique.

Tara Brown is Miriam Webster's undercover name.

Tony Templeton is the Dunes Club's chef.

Valerie Bargewell is a sales clerk at Two.

Vicki Hardman is a sales clerk at Blue Shue.

1

A Body on the Bluff

"CALL 911! CALL the police!" Marty Monroe was out of breath as she ran into the Seaview Cottages community clubhouse and shrieked that command. "There's a body on the bluff!"

"Which one of us is it?" Carl Rodgers hollered. Marty blinked a couple of times without responding. The tall, lanky man in his eighties is a joker. I figured he was kidding, but Marty had come to a complete standstill as if pondering his question. I tried not to plow into her or the other women who were on her heels.

"Not you, obviously, Carl!" Midge Gaylord replied as she veered around Marty and hurried to the reception desk. "You'd better calm yourself down, Marty, or there'll be a body in the clubhouse. I'm calling Deputy Dervish. It's too late for 911. She's already dead."

"No way!" Exclaimed Rosemary Pfeiffer, the receptionist, who had jumped out of her seat. I hadn't seen the cheerful middle-aged woman move that fast since I became a resident a few months ago. She's what folks out here on the West Coast call "laid back." Understanding what "laid back" means is only one of the adjustments I'm trying to make after moving to California from Ohio. I'm not in SoCal—southern California—but north of Santa Barbara on the so-called American Riviera along California's Central Coast.

"Don't tell me it's the newcomer who moved into the Hemingway Cottage a while ago. The woman who wrote the dictionary."

"No, it's not Miriam Webster. Good grief, Carl, I hope you're trying to be funny and not losing your marbles. Miriam's standing right there in the entryway, and she didn't write the dictionary. That's a mnemonic she gave us to help us remember her name since it sounds so much like the famous Merriam-Webster's Dictionary." Midge glanced at me and shook her head in exasperation. That didn't stop Carl.

"I don't need a pneumatic to remember names. What good would a drill do anyway?" Carl gazed at Midge straight-faced, his mouth hanging open a little as if he might genuinely be confused. Midge wasn't buying it. She looked skyward as though praying for strength not to wring his neck.

"Will someone please give Carl a mnemonic to help him remember what a mnemonic is?" Midge was on the phone dialing the local police. She'd tried to call from the bluff area where we'd found the body but had given up. The reception is hit or miss out there amid the sandy hillocks and sparse brush at the edge of a sprawling coastal dune preserve. We'd rushed to the community clubhouse to use the landline instead.

"I haven't written anything, Carl. I'm an *aspiring* writer," I said as I darted past him trying to catch up with

Midge. My dog, Domino, still on her leash, pranced along beside me. Our morning walk had taken a bizarre turn adding to the growing tally of twists in my life over the past year.

"Then it's a good thing you're not dead yet, isn't it?" Carl tugged at a towel draped around his neck. His ruddy complexion was more flushed than usual. He must have just come from the fitness room.

"That's not funny! Miriam's fur baby is standing right there listening to you. Dogs understand more than you might believe. Domino's probably already traumatized since she found the dead woman lying out there near Fitzgerald's Bluff." Penelope Parker spoke in a chiding tone. "Charly" as she preferred to be called in honor of her favorite writer, Charlotte Brontë, was always at the ready to tame Carl's wild side.

Domino was anything but traumatized. She'd growled when she made that gruesome discovery, and then barked wildly which got my attention. I wasn't the only one who had responded to her barking. Domino's urgent cries had summoned several members of the Seaview Cottages Walkers Club who were within earshot. Marty, Midge, Charly, and her dog, Emily, had rushed to join us.

"Don't worry, Charly, Domino's fine. She's still a little wound up given all the excitement." Not as hyper as Emily. Named for another Brontë sister Charly admires, Emily was doing a little tap dance trying to get Domino to play. Domino crouched and kinked her tail, ready to respond to the invitation when Charly scooped Emily up into her arms.

"I would take her back to our cottage, but I don't want

to miss anything." By cottage, Charly meant the Brontë Cottage, another in the Writers' Circle of cottages named after famous authors.

Our Writers' Circle is only one of the residential "Circles" that comprise the Seaview Cottages community. Other Circles honor artists, crafts persons, and luminaries of the theater and cinema. They all pay homage to the "Dunites" who once lived nearby in what is now the Guadalupe-Nipomo Dunes Complex.

The utopian artists' community of Moy Mel, Gaelic for pastures of honey, has all but been erased by sand and time. Once the dunes became a preserve area, a founder's cabin and other remnants were moved to Oceano, so visitors wouldn't damage the dunes.

Oceano is another small town founded on big dreams. At one point, it was slated to become the "Atlantic City of the West" by entrepreneurs aiming to turn it into a vacation mecca. I feel wistful about all the longing and ambition that was never realized. It does make the place I've landed in midlife intriguing, though, and I've just begun to explore its history.

Charly and I must have been as tightly wound as our hounds. We both startled at the sound of a booming voice. Charly yipped making a noise much like the one her excited little Jack Russel Terrier made moments ago.

"My lumbago is killing me!" Joe Torrance griped as he stepped into the enormous lobby from the hallway Carl had traipsed down minutes earlier. Joe held a towel wiping what looked like grease from his hands. "It's always a sure sign there's trouble ahead when the chain comes off the bike."

Shorter than Carl by half a foot, Joe was muscular by comparison. His dark hair and black eyes stood out in contrast to Carl's sandy-gray hair and pale gray eyes. "The odd couple," as we referred to them. The physical differences were only one of many between these two pals.

"That can't be true," Carl huffed.

"Why not? That chain comes off at least once a week now and, for some reason, the rest of my day is usually whacko after that happens."

"Your lumbago can't be killing you. You had it removed last year." Joe didn't say a word. Instead, he shook his head and changed the subject.

"Who's not dead yet?"

"Hemingway," Carl said, pointing to me.

"You're losing it, amigo. That's not Hemingway, it's Miriam who helped write one of the great American dictionaries. I carried a copy of that book with me when I was learning English about a hundred years ago."

Marty, who was now sitting in a comfy armchair waving a brochure back and forth to cool herself, tsk-tsked. Joe's lips twitched as if suppressing a smile. We had another joker in our midst. A quirky sense of humor is one of the things Carl and Joe have in common.

"If you read it about a hundred years ago, how did Miriam help write it? She wasn't even born then." I gulped, hoping the matter of my age wouldn't draw any attention as both men stared at me.

I adjusted the reading glasses I wear, trying to hide the worry in my eyes. Glasses, not covering my gray hair, and going without makeup are strategies I've adopted to appear older. I'll bet I'm one of the only women around who doesn't dye her hair or wear makeup to avoid looking younger. That's part of my strategy to blend in now that I've taken up residence in a fifty-five plus community even though I'm not that old yet.

When my husband, Peter Webster, died unexpectedly last year, he left me in an awful fix. The house we'd lived in for more than twenty-five years was mortgaged to the hilt. Most of our savings were gone, including the money in Pete's IRA that he'd put into "speculative investments."

According to our accountant, his wild schemes had nearly bankrupted us. Neither he nor Pete had bothered to discuss the situation with me. Not even after I lost my job as a bookkeeper when The Pastry Palace shut down.

Maybe Pete had been too embarrassed to discuss our financial difficulties. I know I am. I haven't told a soul about how close to the edge I'm living—another of the secrets I'm keeping. Not using makeup or dying my hair has another advantage—it saves me a few bucks.

Domino tugged at her leash, literally pulling me out of my reverie about the shock and misery of becoming a widow. Emily yelped, and Domino woofed. Joe hadn't said anything in response to Marty's question, but he'd given that towel a snap, putting the dogs back into hyper mode. Emily was squirming so much that Charly had to put her down.

"Will you all please keep it quiet? I'm trying to get Deputy Dervish—" Midge quit speaking mid-sentence and held the phone away from her ear. I could hear the deputy's voice from where I stood a couple feet away. I couldn't make out his words, but I could guess what he was saying. Domino picked up on the tone of the conversation and stepped closer to me. She's a sensitive creature and doesn't like expressions of anger.

"It's okay, girl," I whispered, reaching down to pat her. That set her tail wagging again and put a big doggy smile back on her face.

Midge donned a wicked grin. Then she arched an eyebrow, devilishly, and her brown eyes sparkled. The smile lit up her face ringed by hair that looks like gold-tinged cotton candy. Tormenting the local Sheriff's deputy is one of her favorite pastimes. I'd already witnessed her in action several times. Deputy Devers was no doubt protesting her use of the nickname she has for him. It drives him nuts.

"Why do you call him Deputy Dervish?" I'd asked shortly after I moved in and witnessed my first round of the ongoing sparring match between Midge and the deputy.

"You'll find out soon enough. He's a dirt devil, whirling like a dervish, and stirring up trouble wherever he goes. Ask anyone in Duneville Downs. They'll tell you what a pompous, snot-nosed, no good, troublemaker he is. Not to mention he's ageist, sexist, and every other 'ist' ever invented." That had been Neely Conrad speaking. Neely is short for Cornelia Conrad.

"Now tell us what you really think. Come on! Don't hold back," Midge had said, hoping Neely would continue her rant. Then Midge had offered input of her own about the deputy. "The good thing about all the 'ists' is that it makes him easy to fool. The daffy old dame routine works every time. If you get in a fix, just stand there looking helpless and confused and he'll let it go with a 'Women!'

or a 'Save me from screwy old broads!' statement."

I hadn't seen the plump, bespectacled Neely yet today. That isn't too surprising given that she's a self-proclaimed night owl. "Nothing good happens before noon," she'd said when Midge and a couple other women in the Walkers Club had tried to get her to join them for their morning walks.

An occupant of the Christie Cottage, Neely, loves to read about murder and mayhem into the wee hours of the night. She's not a dog owner, either. Domino would never let me sleep in even if I had stayed up half the night to finish a book.

When Midge spoke again, I hoped it meant she was ready to end the torment and get on with the business at hand. Dirty business, I presume. It's not likely the young, attractive woman we'd found had died from natural causes.

"Look Deputy, I didn't call you to argue. We've got a dead body on our hands." She paused. "No, it's not one of us," Midge said a moment later, rolling her eyes. Then she abruptly quit speaking, put a hand on her hip, and tapped her foot. "Yes, I'm sure. This one's lying behind a bluff down below the Fitzgerald Cottage. A good-looking blonde. Young, too." Midge turned to look at me as she listened to the voice on the other end.

"How do we know what killed her? That's why we called the police!" The deputy must have finally gotten the message. "Uh-huh. Sure. We're in the clubhouse." With that, she hung up the phone and reported to us.

"We've been warned not to go anywhere. Dudley D0-Wrong is on his way." Deputy Dervish obviously isn't

Midge's only misnomer for the local lawman. I haven't witnessed her lampoon the name of Canadian Mountie Dudley Do-Right to irritate the deputy, but I can imagine steam coming out of his ears like a cartoon character! "It won't be long since he was out on the highway arranging to have an abandoned vehicle towed."

Midge had barely finished updating us when Neely stumbled into the clubhouse. It appeared as if she'd thrown on a jacket over her pajamas. She wore slippers and her hair needed to be combed. She scanned the room, looking at each of us before spotting Charly. Even with glasses, Neely's distance vision isn't great.

"Charly, what's going on?" She asked. "I'm sorry I didn't get to the phone in time when you called."

"Not even the second time," Charly said interrupting her. "I take it you did get my voicemail message."

"Yes. I got here as soon as I could. What's this about finding a body?"

"What?" A woman cried out after bursting through the doors. Another resident I recognized strode into the clubhouse moving quickly on a collision course with Neely. It's as if she hit an invisible force field when she heard the word "body," coming up short before running over Neely. Then she looked Neely up and down, zeroing in on her fluffy bedroom slippers with a look of disgust. "What body? Not here in our community, right? Greta's got an open house scheduled for today!"

Even if I hadn't been able to see her, I would have known by the shrill tone of her shrieking voice that it was Alyssa Gardener speaking, half of "*The* Gardeners." She and her husband, Alfred, love calling themselves that given the prize-winning orchids they raise in a greenhouse behind the Potter Cottage. That's not Potter as in Harry Potter, but Beatrix Potter, the beloved writer of Peter Rabbit and other children's stories. Their "Potter's Shed," as they call the greenhouse, is a destination on Greta Bishop's real estate tours with potential homebuyers.

Whoever said gardening was a relaxing hobby sure got it wrong in Alyssa's case. She's the biggest worrywart I've ever met. Even her husband, who prefers to be called Alf, had given up trying to get her to cool it when her hair is on fire. The long-suffering man was at his wife's side in an instant. Like the tortoise and the hare, Alf was often a few strides behind his more frenetic spouse.

A panicky harangue might have been in store for us, except that a series of soft gongs sounded. Chef Tony's breakfast buffet was open. Most days, I prefer making my own breakfast and eating it on the front porch while taking in my view of the Pacific Ocean. It saves money. Chef Tony is a great cook, though, and many 0f the six hundred or so community members enjoy dining in the Dunes Club more often than I do.

That's especially true for golfers with an early tee time. The Seaview Cottages Dunes Course is now a public course. Opening the course to the public was a measure taken to cover the costs associated with its upkeep. It also brings townspeople and tourists to the restaurant. Hungry diners had begun streaming in the moment the restaurant opened as if someone had rung an old triangle chow bell outdoors.

"We'd better go eat, dear, so we don't keep Greta waiting," Alf said, speaking in a calm even-handed tone to his wife, Alyssa. "Can someone fill us in on what's going on?"

"Come on, amigo, it's time to eat." Carl seemed hesitant, but Joe slapped him on the back. "The ladies will catch us up later, won't you?" Midge opened her mouth to speak, probably with some smart aleck retort about his reference to "the ladies." She put a lid on it, though, when the clubhouse door opened again, and a police siren could be heard growing louder by the second.

"Come on Alyssa, we'll tell you what's happened so far," Carl offered. Alf nodded, and a look of relief spread across his face as Alyssa stepped toward the dining room.

"Please keep it down, will you?" Alyssa snipped. "All we need in this community is for word to get out that people are dropping dead here."

"It's not one of us," Carl said. He also said something else that I couldn't hear, but Alyssa did.

"A murder?" She asked in a loud, alarmed voice. A foursome of golfers turned and gazed at her.

"So much for hush-hush," I muttered as she and the men with her disappeared around the corner and down the corridor to the dining room.

"Yeah, I'd say we're all in for more attention like that until this dead body thing gets sorted out," Neely said as she joined Midge, Marty, and me where we stood near the reception desk. "I probably shouldn't run around in my pajamas, should I?" She asked.

"It's too late to go home and change now. You need to stick around to get the details about what's going on," Marty said as the door swung open and Deputy Devers stormed into the lobby. He spotted us and swaggered our way with one hand on his holstered gun as if he might need to draw on us.

"The cavalry has arrived. Try not to swoon, *ladies*," Midge commented in a low voice drenched in sarcasm.

"Brace yourselves for Deputy Devers' version of the third degree since you found the body," Charly added. She gripped Emily tighter as the little dog squirmed.

Great! I thought as I let out an enormous sigh. *More attention is just what I don't need.* I did a quick reality check—something I'd done many times in the past year, trying to keep myself centered in a world spinning out of control around me. I heaved a mighty sigh. At least I'm still alive, unlike the poor dead woman on the bluff.

2

What Body?

"WHERE IS IT?" Deputy Devers asked.

"It was right down there!" Midge exclaimed. Several of us scanned the area below from a vantage point up above the rolling dunes. The trail we were on leads from the overlook where our cottages sit, over the roadway via a small pedestrian bridge, and then down, around, and through a network of smaller bluffs and seaside dunes. It ends at the beach and the blue Pacific Ocean.

"Great! You find a dead body, and then you lose it. Why am I not surprised?" The ever-exasperated deputy took his cap off and wiped his face and then his bald head with a handkerchief. The exertion of walking from the clubhouse, along the pathways that lead out the gates, and down to the bluffs was getting to him.

"You need to get out from behind the wheel of your patrol car more often if you want to keep up with us active adults." Midge's comment drew a grunt from Deputy Devers who, consciously or not, had put his hand back on the holstered gun at his side.

I couldn't see a body anywhere as we moved on down

the trail that led around another mound of dunes. I checked behind each hillock as we wound our way past it, thinking maybe in our shock and confusion, our memories were failing us. Even when we passed Fitzgerald's Bluff, we didn't see a body and kept moving.

A little farther down in front of us, the path widened revealing a view of the beach and foamy waves sliding ashore. That's when I spotted tracks in the sand as if something had been dragged toward the water. I stopped and held both arms outstretched realizing that if we kept moving, we'd tread on those marks, but there must have been footprints earlier. I couldn't see any now. The rising tide or a deliberate attempt to erase them left no obvious prints in the sand.

I pointed them out to my companions and explained what I thought they were. Domino tugged on her leash trying to take me back to a spot we'd just passed. I gave in and backtracked to the hillock we all referred to as Fitzgerald's Bluff which is where I would have sworn we'd seen that body earlier. I checked again. It wasn't there now. Deputy Devers was still farther up the trail and on his satellite phone bellowing.

"Cancel the call you put into the County. We're not going to need anyone out here at 'See-nothing Cottages' after all. There's no body." He paused, apparently listening to the dispatcher. "What do you mean 'another one?' I'm telling you there's not one here. Divert the crime lab guys to Blue Haven."

"That must be where our body went," Charly said loud enough for Deputy Devers to hear. Emily yipped excitedly as if in agreement.

Neely stood next to me shaking one foot trying to get the sand out of her slipper. When that didn't work, she grabbed my arm to steady herself, bent down, and took that slipper off. Sand streamed from it as she turned it upside down.

"It's not *your* body," the deputy snapped responding to Charly's comment.

"We had it first," Midge said, smirking as she spoke. She winked at me, signaling she was well aware of the fact that her statement would irk the deputy. "Is it a young blonde woman? If it is, it's our body. If not, your dispatcher's right and you have another one on your hands."

"I don't have to share that information with you. All I know is that it's the body of a woman."

"Then, Midge is right, and it's ours. That makes more sense than the possibility that we're dealing with two dead women this early in the morning," Marty argued. "I'll bet those folks at Blue Haven aren't happy, are they? You should have gotten here sooner. This is a much better location for a crime scene than on the beach in Snootyville."

"Uh, I'm pretty sure this is still a crime scene," I said as Neely gasped and gave up trying to keep her bare foot out of the sand. When she put it down, she let go of my arm. Then she used the slipper still in her hand to point out an area behind the bluff.

"Deputy Devers, you'd better get the County to send investigators out this way, too," I added. A woman's shoe lay in the sand, half-hidden by a clump of wispy grass. Then I went on alert. There were more items beyond that shoe. Domino reacted to my tension with a woof.

"What is it?" Marty asked.

"Our dead blonde's belongings," I said. "See? That looks to me like a woman's canvas tote with leather straps. Someone's dumped its contents on the sand."

"Your vision beats mine. I'm lucky I could see that shoe. Everything beyond that point is a blur." Neely glanced sideways at me, crinkling up her nose as she checked out my glasses. "Maybe your cheaters are better than my prescription lenses." I gulped. Was it that obvious I was wearing cheap, drugstore reading glasses? I quickly refocused the conversation.

"Body or no body, Deputy, something bad happened here," I remarked.

"Do you think it was a robbery?" Charly asked.

"That's a canvas Gucci sneaker and a Marc Jacobs tote—a grand, easy, lying there in the sand. She could have had some money on her," Marty said as she scrutinized the objects.

"A grand? As in a thousand dollars?" I asked. That would cover three—no, almost four of the car payments I still owe on my hatchback! I felt a tad dizzy at the thought that someone might spend that kind of money on shoes and a handbag.

"Yep! The compact and lipstick are pricey, too, I bet. She could have had jewelry worth stealing, as well as cash and credit cards. I don't remember seeing any jewelry on her, do you?"

"No," I responded.

"I don't either," Midge added. "So maybe this was the scene of a robbery gone wrong although it's an odd place for a mugging to occur."

"If it was a drug deal, a secluded location in the middle of the night or at dawn, might be perfect. It could have turned into a robbery if she had a bunch of money on her. If the drug dealer decided to rob her, and she put up a fight, things could have gotten out of hand fast enough," Charly suggested.

"Is there a wallet?" Neely asked as she took a step forward and bent a little from the waist to get a closer look. I reached out and stopped her before she could take another step.

"Don't touch anything!" Deputy Devers shouted, shoving us aside as he charged down the trail to take over.

"Oh, please," Marty said chiding the deputy. "This stuff has already been lying around for hours exposed to the elements. I'll bet there were lots of footprints before the wind and sand covered them up, instead of just a couple in there where it's sheltered." Marty pointed at what did indeed appear to be footprints.

"Miriam's right," Neely offered. "This is still a crime scene. We shouldn't touch or take anything." Neely spoke to Devers next with an urgent tone in her voice.

"Marty's also got a good point about the deteriorating conditions out here in the open. You'd better tell those guys with the county that they've got a second crime scene to investigate as soon as possible on Fitzgerald's Bluff."

"Will you quit calling it that! This isn't Fitzgerald's Bluff. The only bluff I'm concerned about is that you busybodies with too much time on your hands are playing a silly game."

"Why would we do that?" Midge asked with the phoniest expression of wide-eyed innocence I'd ever seen. She followed with several slow owl-like blinks.

I dropped my chin to my chest hoping to compose myself. A grin wouldn't get Midge to stop or the deputy to move this misadventure along. All I needed was to tick off the local constabulary and get him interested enough to run a background check on me. He wouldn't find much, but my real birthdate and current marital status might be all he'd need to get me into hot water with the Seaview Cottages Homeowner Association.

"How do I know why any of you Seaview Shantytown squatters do what you do?" Midge's mouth popped open. The deputy's comment got to me, too. On one of his previous visits to our community, he'd ranted about how much he yearned to be the one to serve the papers on us when the Seaview Cottages community was put into receivership.

"Good grief!" I exclaimed. "There's one way to find out if this is a prank. Get somebody out here that has some investigative skills to see if there's identification in that tote. Or maybe there's some other information that can be used to link these items to the dead woman they've found at Blue Haven." Deputy Devers' eyes narrowed as he stared at me.

So much for staying on his good side if he has one, I thought. I gave Domino a little tug to keep her close to my side, wishing we'd chosen another route to the beach for her morning walk. A knot formed in my stomach as the deputy continued to stare at me. Then Neely spoke in an annoyed tone.

"No resident of Seaview Cottages is going to pay a thousand dollars to pull a prank on you or anyone else.

Marty was a buyer for high-end department stores for decades before she retired. If she says the shoes and tote cost a thousand dollars, she knows what she's saying." The deputy was about to say something else, but Charly interrupted him.

"You'd better listen to Miriam, Devers. Get somebody out here while there's still evidence to collect. The summer visitors are arriving in droves, and the guides at the Blue Haven Bluejackets Summer Camp sometimes use this path to take their campers to the beach. Mark my words, this stuff won't stay put much longer." Charly was wagging her finger at the deputy as she urged him to act.

"Yeah, this is no game," Marty added. "If any of us had that kind of cash to throw around, we'd put it toward paying off our special assessment for the year."

The knot in my stomach twisted at Marty's mention of a special assessment. I own the Hemingway Cottage outright, but homes in the Seaview Cottages community come with taxes plus monthly homeowner's fees. Another of the surprises I'd discovered once I'd gone through all the paperwork pertaining to my cottage was a notice Pete had received last year. Property owners were now required to pay an extra few thousand dollars in annual special assessments to cover necessary renovations and repairs to common areas that required more funds than the law allowed management to withdraw from the community's reserves. If this dalliance on the dunes didn't end soon, my head was going to explode.

"Why not get the experts out here and let them do their job?" I asked. "You've already trampled the drag marks, and what might also be part of a footprint the killer didn't completely obliterate. See?" I pointed at the ground where he stood. When he'd charged past us earlier, we'd remained up the slope away from those marks, but the deputy had lumbered onto them. "You don't want it to get back to the County that you destroyed evidence at a crime scene, do you?"

"Who knows if that's what they were—uh, are?" The deputy sputtered.

"The crime lab guys will, that's who! If the killer dragged her body down to the water that could explain how she ended up on Blue Haven's beach an hour or so later," I added. I was done mincing words with this guy who Midge had described as dense as a brick. Dense and stubborn.

"Yikes. If you're right, that body must have gone into the water almost as soon as we left," Marty said. The pitch of her voice rose as she realized what that meant.

A creepy pause settled upon us as we scanned the area near where we stood. The trail wound out of sight behind us, and the dunes were piled up high enough on either side of the trail that someone could have hidden nearby. Domino twisted in my grip. Emily woofed.

"You're right, Marty. The killer must have been hiding not far from here to move the body that fast," I said.

"That makes sense," Joe bellowed from behind us. Charly and I both yelped at the sudden sound of a voice coming from a space that had appeared to be devoid of people moments earlier. "Whoa, ladies, I know you're glad to see me, but there's no need to scream like I'm a Rockstar."

"That's twice in one day you've sneaked up on us yelling at the top of your lungs. Two strikes, buddy—three and you're out!" Emily added an exclamation point to Charly's comment with a vertical leap into the air followed by a terse yip.

Joe blinked at Charly without speaking, probably wondering what would happen to him if he struck out. I know I did. When he opened his mouth to ask, Charly's eyes flashed. The petite septuagenarian had her fists balled up and pawed at the ground like a feisty bantam rooster.

"Don't push her. She knows Brazilian jiu-jitsu," Midge warned. Could that be true or was she kidding? Sometimes, Midge was as hard to read as Carl and Joe were. "You two must have shoveled your food down faster than usual," she added.

"We got it to go," Carl said, holding up a takeout bag. He had what looked like a half-eaten fried egg sandwich in his other hand.

"A little bit of Alyssa Gardener goes a long way," Joe added before popping the last bite of a sandwich into his mouth.

"You've got admit that a little bit of us goes a long way, too, Joe. *The* Gardeners invited us to leave when I told Alyssa what you said, Midge. I thought you made a good case that the dead woman was too young to be one of us."

"Why would that upset her?" Midge asked.

"Because he also added a point of his own which I considered to be sound even though it didn't go over well," Joe replied. "Just because the dead woman was young, doesn't take residents off the hook as her killer. Alyssa lost it when Carl said the murderer could be in the

Dunes Club right now. I've never seen anyone alive turn that white before."

"We left while Alf was trying to bring her around." Carl pulled a napkin from his takeout bag and wiped his mouth and hands. Then he reached into the bag again and pulled out a huge glazed donut. My stomach growled. I'd fed Domino before we left for our walk, but I still hadn't had breakfast.

"I bet whoever killed that woman dumped her body in the ocean hoping she'd disappear altogether rather than wash ashore a few miles down the coast," Carl suggested.

"You're right!" Joe exclaimed. "I wouldn't be surprised if the police find a phony note or text message to a friend or family member. Something with a fabricated story saying that she's gone off to Vegas or Baja like in Raymond Chandler's story, *Lady in the Lake*," Joe added.

As the owner of the Chandler cottage, Joe's a huge fan of the noir detective story writer. It was an enthusiasm that Devers apparently didn't share. I guess a little bit of Carl and Joe goes a long way with the deputy, too.

"Will you two just stop! No more pointless speculation. It doesn't matter anyway. No one's going to wonder where she is, note or no note, with her body lying on the beach in Blue Haven," he shouted as he called the dispatcher again. His concession that *their* body was *our* body came with no apology for accusing us of making up a story about finding a body in the first place. Then his eyes narrowed with suspicion. "Maybe you all killed her and dragged her into the ocean since you seem to know so much about what went on here."

"Well, thanks, guys. We've gone from pranksters to

perps. I guess that's progress in Deputy Dervish's whacky world of crime scene investigations. He's no Philip Marlowe, is he?" Midge asked. She didn't wait for a response before asking another question. "If you're right, why would we call you, Devers?"

With that, we were invited to vacate the area. On our way back up the trail, we passed a uniformed officer carrying another of those enormous glazed donuts. He didn't appear to be in a hurry even though he'd been summoned by Deputy Devers to help secure the scene until the crime lab could get a team to the location. Maybe the officer hadn't heard the "make it snappy" part of Devers' order. Midge must have concluded he was lost.

"Down and around to the right," Midge said, pointing the way we had come. "No rush. Enjoy your donut. Deputy Devers has everything under control." With his mouth full, the officer didn't say a word. Instead, he acknowledged Midge with a nod as he sauntered on down the trail.

"I made that up. If he's got it all under control, I'm the Queen of England," Midge said as soon as the officer disappeared. Then she dropped her voice and leaned in to speak. "Am I the only one who's concerned about the fact that there's been a murder this close to the place we all call home?"

An uneasy pause resonated in the silence of the dunes. Even the lapping ocean waves were muted as the trail wound up through the sandy bluffs on either side of us that had grown larger as we walked back toward the roadway and the bridge that would lead us up over it to our gated community.

Joe and Carl were long gone. They'd taken off to find more of those donuts, so it was just the five of us "ladies" and our two happy hounds. I was all done in, but Domino and Emily were fresh as daisies. If Domino had her way, we'd stay out among the dunes or on the beach all day every day.

Even before Midge asked her question about a murder practically on our doorstep, I was more than ready to return to my comfy cottage. I wanted to make sure everything was locked up tight, switch on the alarm system, and make myself a stiff cup of tea.

"*Maybe* a murder," Marty corrected Midge in an almost hopeful tone. "We don't know that for sure yet."

"You may know your high-end fashion accessories, but I know a thing or two about bodies." Midge is a retired nurse who'd spent part of her career in the military. Not on the frontlines, but in Army hospitals where she claims to have seen it all. I believe her. "Petechiae—red marks around her eyes—are almost a sure sign someone murdered her. Strangled her, if I'm right. There were also bruises forming on her neck. I would have pointed them out to the deputy if the dead woman had stayed put."

"Stayed put. Ha!" Charly exclaimed. "What you really mean is if the strangler hadn't sneaked out from a hiding place and dragged her body into the water to get rid of her only moments after we left."

"Too bad we didn't get a look at the rat before he or she scurried out of there," I groused. "At least then we'd have some idea of which diner at the Dunes Club to avoid."

"A body on the bluff, a killer on the loose, and enough

loot lying in the dirt to pay my annual special assessment. This morning sucks," Neely moaned. "I should have stayed in bed!"

"You did! At least your dilly-dallying means the killer didn't get a look at you like he did the rest of us who have now become strangler bait," Midge snorted.

"Strangler bait with Deputy Devers on the job!" Marty cried. "We're doomed!"

"Not necessarily," Charly said, stopping suddenly and placing both hands on her hips as we stopped for a moment and stood on the bridge. "Let's talk this over at dinner—my house—not the Dunes Club. I'll make my Queen City Chili and you each bring a dish."

"If Miriam will make dessert, it's a deal!" Neely said. When she started walking again, we followed her. I was relieved to be moving again. I'd felt way too exposed standing there on the bridge like that. What if we were being watched?

"Dessert it is!" I exclaimed, trying to muster enthusiasm and tamp down my mounting paranoia. "I love the Cincinnati version of Queen City Chili. Count me in."

The meat chili, made with a slightly exotic blend of Middle Eastern spices, had been one of Pete's favorites. Poured over steaming spaghetti, smothered in cheese, and then topped with onions and beans, he loved Queen City Chili served five-way, as they call it in Ohio. My husband enjoyed his life and lived it with great gusto! Food was a big part of that, and I still miss cooking for him.

All those years as the bookkeeper for The Pastry Palace had left me with an almost insatiable urge to bake—even after I lost my job there. The drive only grew stronger after

Pete died and the life we'd lived for more than twenty-five years had ended abruptly.

I hadn't spent all my time in the back office keeping the books. In fact, I'd picked up skills as a baker and had gained access to more than enough heavenly recipes to bake my way into a sugary oblivion. In my effort to fill the void Pete left in my life, I shared the sweet treats I baked with family, friends, and neighbors. They soon began coming to me with requests for their favorite goodies. If I hadn't been up to my eyeballs in debt, I might have tried to set up a shop. I learned to whip up treats for almost any occasion—special or otherwise. My mind whirred into action flipping through the file of recipe cards stored in my head. The stash I had stored online was much larger.

What would it take to sweeten up this mess? I wondered.

3

Home Sweet Home

As I OPENED the door for Domino, I sighed, realizing Midge was probably right that we'd have little help from authorities anytime soon. I gave Domino a treat for being such a good girl—a small sliver of the bacon I put on a plate to go with fresh berries, a lemon poppy seed muffin, and a cup of tea.

"Breakfast at last!" I mumbled as I slipped into a comfy seat in the cozy cottage I now call home. My Hemingway Cottage didn't feel quite as cozy after what we'd been through this morning. Nor was the chair as comfy as it had been before last night when I'd sat in it and pored over the Seaview Cottage Community's Homeowner Association accounts.

When I moved to Seaview Cottages, members of the "HOA," as they call it around here, had asked me to join the finance committee. The papers Pete had filled out when he bought the house designated my occupation as a bookkeeper. I didn't want to be on the committee, but to avoid ruffling any feathers I did as they asked. I hadn't corrected the misunderstanding about my marital status when the HOA President told me how much he was looking forward to seeing Pete again.

The conversation this morning about extra assessments added to the anxiety I'd felt after reviewing the community's books. I'm not alone living on the edge of a financial cliff. There's no doubt in my mind the community needs to raise the extra cash those special assessments would bring in over the next few years. I'd have to find a way to cough up my share since I can't afford to lose the cottage now that I've made it my home.

In addition to a death benefit I receive as Pete's widow, I have my own small IRA, but I can't get to it until I'm fifty-nine and a half. Money's tight. At least until I can find a job in Duneville Downs or another nearby town.

I'd already begun looking, but so far, I'd spotted only one opening for a bookkeeper. I dread the thought of filling out an application where I'm required to indicate my age and marital status. In a small town, people talk about newcomers. It's not a good idea to lie on a job application, but telling the truth puts me in a pickle with the HOA.

"Oh, the tangled web we weave..." I chanted quietly. Domino, who'd positioned herself at my feet, raised her sleepy head to check on me. "It's okay, girl. Your momma's just pondering the trouble she's in now that she's practicing 'to deceive.'" With a few quick wags of her tail, Domino dropped her head down and resumed her nap.

I hadn't given much thought to what it would be like day-to-day, living with my silly secrets. Moving to the West Coast hadn't been my first choice as a solution to my problems. I'd tried to sell the cottage to raise cash and rid myself of debts. After going over the books, I now understand why no one had been eager to purchase my lovely little cottage on a quiet street overlooking the Pacific Ocean and just steps away from a golf course.

Given the community's aging infrastructure and financial troubles, only a quixotic dreamer like my poor dead husband would have bought a home here. I'm sure he'd seen the place for what it had been or could be rather than what it is. There is a charm about the place and the setting is lovely, but that hadn't been enough to interest buyers.

Potential buyers must have been smarter than Pete was about the community's financial challenges. Money was never Pete's forte. I could have weighed in on the matter if my seemingly straightforward husband had been less secretive.

After Pete died, I tried to recall if I'd missed hints that we were sliding toward financial ruin. Two issues came to mind. When I'd lost my job, Pete had assured me that I'd find another job soon. There had been something in the way he'd said it that I'd missed at the time. I now recognized that his comment might have been meant less as a vote of confidence in my skill and experience as a bookkeeper, and more as an impetus to urge me on in my job search. Especially the "soon" part.

The second issue had been his reluctance to sit down and plan with me as my unemployment money ran out and I still hadn't found another job. At that point, he hadn't appeared worried in the least. In fact, he'd been upbeat. In hindsight, I figure he must have been riding high on the prospect that one of his schemes was about to pay off. Why hadn't I been more insistent or investigated our finances without his participation when he stalled? I trusted him, that's why.

In any case, it's clear to me now that I didn't know the man as well as I thought I did. He'd hidden plenty from me. One of the secrets I carry around with me—one that still hurts a year after Pete's death—is that he'd signed my name to loan papers, borrowing money against the equity in our house. I couldn't bring myself to tell anyone because I'd have to say words like that out loud. I'd hemmed and hawed about it, even when my sister had asked me point blank about my finances.

"What could she or anyone else have done about it at that point?" I asked in a whisper. Domino sat up and scooted close enough to put a paw on my lap, and looked up at me with her dark, soulful puppy eyes. "Ah, you're a good girl. We're doing just fine, Domino!"

For now, at least. After trying to sell the Hemingway Cottage for six months, I'd given up. Living here beats paying rent on top of the expenses related to maintaining the cottage. Unfortunately, here I am at fifty, residing in a community for people aged fifty-five and over, and without my older spouse who would have made that okay. So much for keeping a low profile now that I'd been pulled into the brouhaha surrounding a body on the bluff.

Just then, a breeze blew in through the open sliders that lead to a small backyard. The salty air tinged with verbena reminded me, once again, that the place I'd landed in my widowhood isn't so bad. I stood up and sucked in great gulps of the ocean breeze. Domino followed me as I walked to the open sliding door and peered outside.

The California Bungalow style house, built in the seventies, has a covered porch out front that's great for viewing the ocean. It also has a backyard and a tiny slab patio. Small in comparison to the one behind our house in Ohio, it's far better than no yard as I learned while living in a rental apartment that had no outdoor space for Domino.

The yard is enclosed by a white picket fence that I'd given a new coat of paint soon after moving in. My DIY paint job had revealed that the fence isn't very sturdy. It's also low enough that Domino could jump it and take off if she decided to go for it.

A leap like that would give her access to the well-kept greens of the golf course. As I gazed at the rolling links with their white sand bunkers and scruffy roughs, a golf cart whirred into view. This one wasn't out on the greens, but on the cart path that wound behind our cottages.

My anxious mind that had finally settled down went back on high alert when the golf cart came to a halt. The man behind the wheel stepped from it, looked around him as if trying to determine if anyone was watching. Then he scanned the cottages and began taking pictures on a cellphone. On any other morning, I might have written off the behavior as that of an avid golfer longing for a cottage on the course. Or maybe a curious "looky-loo" checking out the property. Not today!

"This calls for action, Domino!" I exclaimed, grabbing my phone and calling Midge, who was probably in the cottage closest to the guy in the cart.

"Hello," she said, answering on the first ring.

"Midge, look out your sliders, will you? Do you see the golf cart parked on the path? The driver's taking pictures."

"And so am I," Midge responded. "I'm going to hang up and take more. Call Neely, will you? She's got the best head on view of that cart. The club tags them. We might be able to find out who's using it today if she can get a good enough picture of the tag." She didn't even wait for a response from me before she ended the call. I didn't hesitate, either. Like Midge, I had Neely on speed dial, along with half a dozen residents with whom I spoke often.

"Neely," I said the second she said hello. "It's Miriam. Go to your sliders and look at the guy in the golf cart."

"So?" She responded.

"Shoot!" I said when I realized he'd climbed back into the cart and had started moving. I was about to say "never mind" when he stopped again. Closer to me this time, he got out of the cart, did that furtive scan of his surroundings, and started snapping photos.

"Well, I'll be a blue-nosed gopher! If he's a killer hunting us down, he's a brazen one, isn't he?"

"Midge wants you to try to get a picture of the tag on the front of the golf cart. Can you do that? Does your phone take photos?"

"I can do better than that. I've got my trusty camera right here with a telephoto lens. I use it for birdwatching. Let's see if it can help nail us a jailbird. I'll transfer the photos to my phone and bring them along with me to dinner at Charly's."

"Don't take any chance that he'll see you. There's no reason to add your face to his collection if he's the killer who nabbed the rest of us snooping around out on the bluff," I warned.

"I will. I'm not anxious to become strangler bait. Bye!"
Neely responded in an excited tone, followed by a low
chuckle. I couldn't believe she was enjoying this.

Then, like a moth to the flame, I found myself drifting
closer to the back door. Neely's comment about the
boldness of the fellow suddenly irked me. I moved close
enough to the glass sliders that I could almost have left a
nose print on them. I quietly opened the screen a few
inches to get the clearest view possible of the stranger and
snapped away.

"Take that!" I said in a whisper as if I were firing
buckshot at him rather than capturing his dubious
character in pixels. When he began to move again, I kept
clicking away until he screeched to a halt and peered
directly at me. I shrank back from view, flattened myself
against the wall. Domino, who had been observing my
strange behavior, jumped up. She ran to the door put a
paw into the opening of the screen door, slid it wide open,
and bounded out into the backyard barking wildly.

"Good job, Miriam," I said. "You, crafty sleuth!"
Even if the killer hadn't seen me clearly at Fitzgerald's
Bluff, there's no way he could have missed Domino. If the
guy in the golf cart's our strangler out on the prowl, he
now knows where the big spotted dog and its owner live.

"Domino, come here, sweetie!" I said in a hushed tone
and then peeked out. The cart was gone—moving at a
good clip heading toward the Bogart Cottage in the
"Cinema Circle." Domino was celebrating her rout of the
fellow by bounding from one side of the yard to the other.
When she heeded my call, she stood at my feet wagging
her tail furiously.

"Good girl!" I said as I bent down, took her head in both hands, and rubbed her soft ears. "You sent that bad man running, didn't you?" She pointed her nose skyward and woofed as if bursting with pride at my praise. Then I had a good laugh, hoping it hadn't been some poor golfer after all. Our resident realtor, Greta Bishop, would be furious if Domino and I had just chased off a would-be homeowner. Her job couldn't be an easy one given the challenges facing our community.

"I bet you scared the living daylights out of that guy! That'll teach him to roam the grounds without Bishop Greta at his side." "Bishop Greta" was another of Midge's snarky pet names for people. It fit. Greta's offer to shake my hand when we met had been made with her hand held at an angle that suggested I might want to kiss her ring.

"Strangler bait," I harrumphed. If that's what I'd become, I wasn't going to stand idly by and watch while the rat planned his next move. "I choose Death by Chocolate," I said in a loud voice suddenly realizing what I was going to bake for dessert tonight. "Come, Domino. A brave dog like you deserves a treat. My brave friends do, too."

That statement brought me up short. Despite my plan to remain standoffish given all the secrets I was keeping, I really had made quite a few friends, hadn't I? Quirky, with foibles, but funny and feisty—just the way I like them. They'd appreciate the idea of Death by Chocolate Cake as a twisted take on the events of the day.

"Wait until they taste it, Domino," I murmured. "They'll be tempted to believe they've died and gone to heaven!" Domino's tail thumped the floor where she'd plopped down.

I hit play on my mini-stereo system. It's set up on display shelves that serve as a divider between the kitchen and the living area. I like the open design of the cottage, but I'm not the neatest person when I bake. The shelves make it harder for someone who comes to the door to see if the kitchen's covered in a dusting of flour.

I used a big wooden spoon as a microphone to sing along with Annie Lennox as she raged about the loss of sweet dreams. That song had been almost too poignant the first time I belted out the words after Pete died. I'd started playing all sorts of music to keep the house from seeming too quiet. If Domino's any judge, I'm not much of a singer.

I took a couple of quick steps, sidled up to the oven, turned it on, and set the temperature. Then I began pulling items from the fridge and cupboards, moving with the beat. When I did a quick spin, Domino woofed, stood up and mimicked me. She loves my dancing.

As the cottage filled with delightful aromas, my mind bounced back and forth between worry and anticipation. While the cake layers baked, I mixed the frosting, and then cleaned up my mess. When I pulled the chocolatey layers of cake from the oven, I felt a wave of anticipation about the evening.

What did Charly have in mind when she suggested we get together and talk things over? We'll have even more to talk about now that we had photos to share of the cagey gentleman in the golf cart we'd caught spying on us. If that's what he was doing. He sure had taken off in a hurry once Domino barked at him. Would we learn anything useful about him from those photos? Even if Neely got a good enough picture of the tag the golf club had put on the cart, could we get someone to tell us who had used that cart today?

That's when it dawned on me I hadn't even examined the pictures I'd taken with my phone. A tingle of excitement ran through me. What if the guy in that golf cart was a resident? Maybe I could find him in one of the Seaview Cottages online photo albums. As a member of the HOA Finance Committee, I also have access to archived files that include more photos. The cake needed to cool before I could slather it with ganache and then frost it, so why not take a few minutes to see if I could I.D. the guy?

After setting a timer and fortifying myself with another cup of tea, I settled in at the kitchen table with my laptop. I was so focused on identifying the man in those photos, I forgot all about the alarm I'd set to tell me the cake was cool enough to frost. When it pinged, my heart raced. It wasn't just the sudden sound of the alarm that had my heart revved up; I'd found the guy in the golf cart!

"He's a good-looking man," I said. Domino lifted her head and did this cute thing she sometimes does—tilting her head to one side as if she didn't quite understand or believe what I was saying. "Oh, stop! I'm not over Pete yet, you know that."

Was that true? I wondered. I'd caught myself looking at men a few times lately. Mostly, when I'd encountered a man wearing a friendly smile or commenting on a subject I found intriguing. Still, the very idea of anything like dating was too overwhelming to consider. Especially after the disastrous surprise blind date my sister sprang on me one night at dinner in a last-ditch effort to keep me in Ohio. That had been awkward and embarrassing for me and the guy with whom it became apparent I had nothing in common.

"Besides, he's way too young for me. Couldn't you tell that when you sent him packing, Domino?" I asked as I examined the photos again. My sweet girl tilted her head the other way and then woofed. "You're absolutely correct! He's not too young for the dead woman you discovered this morning, is he?"

I'd read somewhere that women are most often murdered by a spouse or a boyfriend. Was our all-too-curious golfer an angry boyfriend who'd strangled her in a fit of jealousy or after a bad break up? Given my guess that he was barely in his forties, I doubted he was a resident. Nor would he be eligible to purchase property in here anytime soon. He could have gained admission to the community by using the public golf course.

What was he doing then? Was he checking the cottages, Circle by Circle, searching for us? Why? Surely, he wasn't a mass murderer planning to kill us all.

"Not very stealthy for a strangler hunting his next victim," I murmured, suddenly feeling silly about my unwarranted suspicion of a man I'd never met. In my defense, it's not every day you stumble upon a dead body. "Enough! It's time to put the icing on the cake."

4

Dinner and a Murder

CHARLY'S COTTAGE IS a well-organized version of a "hoarder's" home. She admits she has a hard time throwing things away. The woman has lots of hobbies that include reading, watercolor painting, crocheting, and who knows what else? Brazilian jiu-jitsu if Midge wasn't joking this morning.

I'm sure having Emily around didn't help either. The energetic dog met me at the door with a toy for me to toss. When I did that, she was back in a flash, but with a different toy, the other one still where I'd thrown it.

"I spent the afternoon cleaning up," Charly said when I stepped into the foyer and followed her past the cozy living room to the kitchen at the back of the house. It really was more orderly than I'd seen it on my two previous visits. Bookshelves stood in every room, loaded not just with books, but also with souvenirs acquired during her travels around the world.

I'm curious, but I have no idea what Charly did before she retired two decades ago. Many of the retirees in the Seaview Cottages community prefer to talk about what they're doing now rather than reminisce about their pasts.

That's fine with me. Given my reluctance to disclose much about my background, I don't press anyone about anything.

My cottage is a study in Midwest comfort with a few coastal touches I've added trying to get in sync with the seaside setting. By contrast, Charly's house is exotic. Not only in the visual sense exuded by African masks hanging on the walls, ornate brass figurines of Indian gods and goddesses, or oddly shaped drums and other musical instruments tucked away in one corner of her den. Fragrances floated through the air conjuring up fanciful images of spice-filled marketplaces and ancient temples. Patchouli incense, maybe. Leather-bound books neatly lined up in one bookcase cast their scent, too, as did a basket full of wood that must have included chunks of cedar and some other aromatic wood.

Charly didn't broadcast her taste for the exotic in her grooming or attire. Her dark brown hair, streaked with gray, was clipped short. The bob framed her face, drawing you in to an adventurous sparkle in her dark eyes. The black teardrop earrings she wore, with a black embroidered poetess blouse over tan ankle length pants, conveyed a hint of vintage romance—like that in her beloved Brontë sisters' books.

"Ah, there it is!" Charly exclaimed as we took a quick detour into a guest room she uses as her study. She grabbed a tall glass half full of ice. "I need more lemonade. Let me pour you some, too, okay?"

"Sounds wonderful," I said as I eyed the inviting brew that had a rosy pink color. "What gives it that color?"

"Opal basil. I enjoy it, but it's sweetened with basil

syrup. You can have fizzy water if you'd prefer." Her eyes dropped to the cake carrier in my hands. "You have no fear of sugar, do you?"

"Maybe I should, but I can't imagine life without it. After all the years I worked at The Pastry Palace, I developed a real sweet tooth."

"You only live once. Why not enjoy life? So long as no one gets hurt and you can get away with it." She gave me a conspiratorial look that I hope was about whatever she had planned for this evening. Could she be on to me about my age or the fact that my husband was no longer alive? No one had asked me for proof of age when I moved in since Pete had done that when he closed on the house.

The HOA rules are clear about occupancy being re-stricted to those fifty-five or older. In the case of married couples, only one member must be fifty-five and both our names are on the deed. No one has asked any questions about the fact that I now pay the HOA dues and Peter Webster is nowhere to be seen.

When I followed Charly into the kitchen to get the lemonade, I was engulfed in a spicy aromatic cloud. From the chili, no doubt, bubbling in a pot on the stove. I detected a hint of allspice—a dead giveaway that this was no ordinary chili.

A wave of nostalgia hit me. Pete loved Skyline's Queen City Chili so much, I'd searched the web and practiced until I came up with a reasonably good copycat recipe. I wish he were here to enjoy Charly's version with me.

The doorbell jolted me out of my reverie. Charly hand-ed me a glass of lemonade as she ran to answer the door. Emily zoomed ahead of her, making little clicking sounds with her toenails as she ran to greet the new arrival.

"Please put dessert on the breakfast bar. There's room right next to the dessert plates." She paused as she left the kitchen and pointed to a stack of small gold-rimmed dessert plates in a brightly colored paisley print.

When Charly returned, she had Midge and Marty in tow. They all stopped when they saw the cake I'd unveiled. Their mouths fell open.

"What is that?" Marty asked.

"Three layers of chocolate cake with ganache filling sandwiched in between the layers. It's all covered with a fudgy frosting before topping the iced cake with chocolate chips, and then drizzled it with melted chocolate chips."

"Layers upon layers of chocolate," Charly said. "I could swoon."

"That's why it's called Death by Chocolate," I said with a wicked grin on my face.

"What a way to go!" Midge proclaimed.

"Better than what happened to Diana Durand, that's for sure." We all turned to see Neely standing there. Apparently, the discussion about that cake had released enough endorphins that Neely's stealthy arrival didn't trigger a yelp from any of us. "You left the door unlocked, Charly. That's not a good idea under the circumstances."

"Sorry. I'm not used to being strangler bait," Charly replied.

"Neely's not just concerned about what went on this morning. Wait until we tell you what happened this afternoon," Midge added, glancing at me as she said that. Charly and Marty both stared at us.

"We had a mysterious visitor," I said. "Midge, Neely,

and I will tell you all about him."

"How interesting," Charly commented. "Let's eat before we get down to the business of discussing murder most foul and mysterious visitors."

"Interesting to you, maybe, but I'll take my boring life back, thank you very much." Marty sighed.

"I love the idea of fortifying ourselves with food first. Chili and chocolate—yum!" Neely, her unruly curls held in check with an ornate cloisonné hairpin, swished past me. The brightly colored caftan she wore swirled about her. I hadn't seen women wearing those since the 1970s, but this is California.

In Neely's case, it's most likely a holdover from her time in the theatrical community. She'd been an actress in her younger days and then moved into the business of costumes and makeup. That had included stints behind the scenes in regional theaters and in a few big screen Hollywood productions. She has a flare for the dramatic whether she's in a silk caftan or her PJs and slippers.

Dinner was enjoyable even though I deflected the conversation onto others a couple of times when I feared someone was getting close to asking me questions about my marriage. At one point, I caught Charly staring at me with an arched eyebrow making me worry once again that she was somehow on to me. Perhaps, she'd detected that I was purposely being evasive.

The chili was delicious, served with the cornbread Neely had brought, and a salad Marty had whipped up. Even though we were already full, we dug into the cake. With a cup of decaf coffee, the rush of sugar and chocolate set the perfect mood to tackle the day's events.

"According to this news story, Diana Durand is the dead woman's name. Here's her photo, see?" Neely turned her tablet around, so we could all get a look at the image.

"That's her!" I said. "It's the woman Domino found this morning."

"Yes, it is," Midge agreed. "I bet she's not more than twenty-five in that picture."

"The photo must be a recent one. It's from her employee's badge at the Blue Haven Resort," Neely said. "In the article with this picture, it says she was a saleswoman at the resort's Blue Moon Boutique."

"'Was a local woman's Siren's Song her undoing?' What does that headline mean?" Midge asked as she peered over Neely's shoulder and read that title aloud.

"One of Diana Durand's coworkers said that's probably what got her killed and the reporter ran with it, I guess. According to the loquacious former *'friend,'* who asked to remain anonymous, Diana was a nightclub singer from the Bay Area who used her skills as a songstress to lure men to their ruin."

"Swan song's more like it," I muttered.

"Who needs enemies with friends like that?" Marty added. "If I were the police, I'd have that nasty so and so at the top of my list of suspects. Envy's as good a reason as any to kill someone."

"Catty remarks, yes, but they don't sound angry or threatening," Charly said in an authoritative way. "Besides, if the coworker's right, there could be more than one man out there with a motive to silence the songbird."

"Or a woman could have had it in for her if one of the men Diana Durand led astray dumped his old flame for her," Neely suggested. "She would have had to be big or full of fury to drag Diana's body down into the water."

"Not all men could have handled a feat like that, either," I muttered, halfway speaking to myself. "A man or woman angry enough to strangle Diana could have done it in a rush of adrenalin. That's what you're getting at, right, Neely?"

"Yes, that's what I meant," Neely replied. "Moving the body had to have happened posthaste once you all left to call the police. Maybe there's still a footprint down there that can help the investigators determine whether the killer was a man or woman. I'll concede that it would have been easier for a man to do the deed in a hurry."

"Did the friend happen to name any of the men Diana supposedly lured to their ruin?" I asked.

"Not in the article," Neely replied as she scanned it again.

"I bet I could find that out." All our eyes were suddenly on Marty.

"You could? How?" Midge asked. Marty didn't respond right away. She appeared to be a bit shy, or anxious perhaps, after blurting out that offer to help.

"I know the woman who used to manage the store where Diana worked. She was my contact at the Blue Moon Boutique when I was still employed as a buyer. Donna Wolz is retired now, like me, but she keeps up with what goes on at the shop. At all the resort shops, in fact. If she doesn't have the scoop on Diana Durand's men friends, she'll know who does."

"Are you sure you're okay with the idea of doing that?" Neely asked, still studying Marty's face. She now wore a worried expression despite the fact she'd sounded emphatic about being able to get information about the men involved with Diana Durand.

"Well, it feels a little risky." Marty shrugged. "I'm willing to give it a try."

"Why not? Do you imagine that Deputy Devers is going to figure anything out? That article also says the autopsy's still pending, but the police are treating her death as a homicide. I don't need an autopsy to tell me someone strangled her. Whoever did it is still out there free as a bird." Neely sighed, and then nodded as she spoke again.

"Unfortunately, that's all true. Meanwhile, we had a mysterious visitor this afternoon, as Midge already knows. Free as a bird is one thing, circling like a hawk is quite another! I'm as dubious as you are about the deputy's investigative abilities. What I'm suggesting is that we consider the risks, proceed with caution, and none of us gets too far out of our 'comfort zone.' Especially not if we're out snooping alone." Neely adjusted her glasses and then filled in Marty and Charly about our encounter with the all-too-curious golfer.

"A perfect stranger somehow believes it's okay to creep around, spying on us. How do you like that?" Marty asked, her blue eyes glaring in anger. Gone was any hint of timidity in the petite woman who sometimes reminded me of a sixty-something Dame Judi Dench. As if on cue, she delivered a dramatic line. "How dare he!"

"Apparently, our mystery man's not a stranger to everyone in our community," I offered as I explained what I'd done once I had a photo of the nosy golfer. "I'm certain

Greta Bishop can tell us more about him. By the way she's leaning in and smiling at him at a holiday gathering at the clubhouse, I'd say they're on friendly terms." It was my turn for show and tell as I displayed the photo I'd put on my cell phone.

"See?" I said, handing the phone to Charly. Charly took a turn peering at the seemingly amiable and attractive well-dressed man, and then passed it along to Marty who slipped on the glasses dangling from a chain around her neck, peered at the image, and immediately calmed down.

"That's a relief," she said, removing her glasses. "If he was hanging out with Greta, maybe he was scouting properties and not trying to find his next murder victim."

"It could be. There's one way to find out. If Greta or someone else who was at that event can tell us who he is, we might get a better handle on why he was checking out our cottages this afternoon." I took my phone back, wondering which one of us might have the best chance of getting Greta to answer a few questions about the man she'd found so charming at that holiday affair.

"If he's a strangler, at least he's good-looking," Marty added. "Too young to be one of us."

"Not necessarily. He could be a resident if he's married and his spouse is over fifty-five," Midge said.

"That's possible, but I can't believe that at least one of us wouldn't have been introduced to him if he was married to one of our community members," Charly commented as she examined the image of the man again. "He's not the kind of man you'd forget, is he?"

"I agree. He exudes the confidence of a man who's out to make an impression on everyone in the room! Here's another idea. The HOA Executive Committee took a new look at the eighty/twenty rule, right? Given how chummy he and Greta appear to be, maybe he's new to the community and got in here that way even though he's not fifty-five," Neely added.

"What's the eighty/twenty rule?" I asked, perking up a little hearing there might be a way around the fifty-five minimum age requirement.

"Age restricted communities can allow exceptions to the fifty-five plus requirement for up to twenty percent of residents. Communities like ours have been looking at the option to help sell properties since the real estate market crashed ten years ago."

I felt a flutter of hope that there might be a way out of the little cloud of white lies that had engulfed me in my widowhood. So far, they're lies of omission rather than commission, but guilt and paranoia-inducing for an old Catholic-school-girl like me. Midge's next comment shut the door on that hope.

"That can't be, Neely. So far, the committee members haven't reached agreement about a policy change. Even our resident realtor opposed the idea, so I doubt he or anyone else has been granted a waiver to live here without a partner or spouse who's fifty-five or older."

I tried not to allow my disappointment to show. Charly, who had been rather quiet as we discussed the still unnamed golfer, was watching me again. I felt like a specimen under a microscope. The slight tilt of her head reminded me of Domino's quizzical expression. Unlike Domino, she could do more than woof if she had questions. It was time to get the conversation moving again.

"Okay, so we have a few things we can do to find out if this guy is our strangler. Did you get a picture of the tag on the cart he was driving, Neely?"

"I sure did. Why don't we ask Joe about it? He helps in the garage at the Dunes Course—fixes the carts when they break down. I'm sure he can get us the name of the person who reserved that cart."

"That's a great idea," I said. "If he gets us a name, maybe it'll match one Marty gets from her friend, Donna. If it turns out this guy knew the dead woman and was hanging around here today, that might be enough information for the police to take a close look at him. We need to act quickly if this guy really is stalking us."

"That won't happen if we take it to Deputy Devers," Midge groused. "I don't think 'act quickly' is in his playbook—especially not if the information comes from a group of daffy old dames!"

"Who says we have to give the information to Devers?" Neely asked. "Remember? The news article said Diana Durand's death is being investigated as a homicide. That must mean her case has been turned over to the County Sheriff's Violent Crimes unit."

"That would be great, if it's true!" Marty exclaimed. "We could do a little bit of legwork and then turn this awful mess over to the proper authorities. End of story! I love that idea. I'll contact my friend tomorrow and see what she can tell us about Diana Durand and the men in her life."

"Neely's on the right track about a way to avoid a confrontation with Deputy Devers." Charly's eyes rested on Midge when she made that comment. "I'll use my contacts to find out who's handling the case at the County Sheriff's office. That way we can avoid going through the deputy altogether."

I'll admit that I was now gazing at Charly in much the same way she'd stared at me earlier. No one seemed surprised by the fact that she had "contacts" that gave her access to police authorities. I wanted to ask about it, but what if she returned the favor with questions about me?

"If you want to speak to Joe tomorrow morning, Neely, I'll go with you. I'll bring the pictures I have of the guy and we can show those to him along with the tag number you have on the golf cart."

"Let's do it!" She exclaimed.

"You bring the pictures you have of Diana Durand from the news story along, too. We can drop by the Clubhouse and ask Rosemary if she's seen either of them. She might be the one who arranged for him to attend that holiday dinner event at the Dunes Club where he's chatting with Greta."

"That's possible, isn't it?" Marty asked.

"If he and Diana were a couple, maybe they had dinner at the Dunes Club some night. We could talk to Chef Tony," Neely added.

"Yes! Or maybe he and Greta were in there together at some point. We can check with the seating hostess and servers, too—sort of make the rounds, you know? Keeping it low key, of course." Gears in my head whirred wondering what that meant in terms of how we approached people with our questions. "If people ask, why do we say we care?"

"Oh, my, you are new to Seaview Cottages, aren't

you? This place thrives on gossip. I'll be very surprised if you don't get cornered the minute you step into the clubhouse. If not by Rosemary, then someone else who wants to hear everything you have to say about finding a body on Fitzgerald's Bluff."

"How early in the morning?" Neely asked. "I'm going to need my wits about me to play the part of a stealthy sleuth." I laughed when she pretended to use a magnifying glass to snoop at her surroundings.

"I don't know—how about ten or ten-thirty? That way we miss the breakfast rush in the dining room and get our questions answered before the lunch crowd arrives." Neely nodded.

"Okay. I can handle ten-thirty. Come by and pick me up, okay? I promise I won't be wearing my pajamas." That provoked a round of laughter.

"You'd be in big trouble if you ran into *The* Gardeners like that again. She'd report you to Greta for driving down our precious property values."

"I hope Greta comes after me. I'd love to ask what she and our mystery man in the photo were chatting about." Neely folded her arms defiantly.

"You know what? You and Miriam have enough to do. Why not let me try to track Greta down? I'll ask her that very question if you two can send me photos of Diana Durand and the man Greta's drooling over."

"If you wait until after I call my friend, I'd love to go with you, Midge. I'd never confront Greta alone about any of this, but I'd sure like to see how she reacts when you show her the picture of the handsome strangler."

At that point, Charly took charge. Perhaps, she'd been

holding back, not wanting to push any of us to become an amateur sleuth at her provocation. In a few more minutes, we each had our assignments for the next day. Charly, too, since she was committed to getting as much inside information as possible from her sources at the County Sheriff's Department—including learning what she could about any evidence collected out around Fitzgerald's Bluff or on the beach at the Blue Haven Resort.

We'd made our decision. Our tasks were clear. We were ready to act. If there's anything I'd learned in the past year, though, it's how often the plans we make and actions we take have unintended consequences. I braced myself, wondering what surprises we'd face tomorrow. What could be more surprising than a body on the bluff?

5

Resident Sugar Daddy

THE NEXT MORNING, Neely and I set out to do as we'd planned. Joe wasn't around, so we started our round of conversations in the clubhouse by speaking to the receptionist first. Rosemary recognized the guy immediately. When I handed her my cell phone with that photo on it, she even remembered which holiday event he was attending based on the decorations in the background.

"I've seen him a couple of times, but I don't know his name. I can look and see if it's on Greta Bishop's holiday reservation as a plus-one, if you'd like."

"Would you, please?" I asked.

"Sure. What's your guess about his name?"

"What?"

"I love trying to guess a person's first name just by looking at them. I'm pretty good at it too. He's hot, isn't he? A square jaw, big smile with sparkling white teeth, broad shoulders, and a full head of neatly cut hair. That's a nice suit, too, isn't it? I'm going to say his name is John—more Jon Hamm than John Wayne, given how polished he is."

I was having trouble keeping up with the perky woman

wearing earrings that sported images of Marilyn Monroe. Among other things, Rosemary is a dedicated movie buff. Not surprisingly, she helps organize and attends many of the events sponsored by residents of the Cinema Circle cottages. I'm sure I had a blank expression on my face.

"J-o-n—as in Jon Hamm," she said again. "The star of *Mad Men*—you must know that series, right?"

"Oh, sure." I'm familiar with the series and the actor; I just wasn't sure where the conversation was going. Neely must have had a similar concern.

"So, is his name, John, or J-o-n or what?" Neely asked.

"Uh, let me see. Sorry. Greta brought a plus one, but there's no name on her reservation request. JoAn might know. You want me to ask her?"

"That's not necessary," I replied, hoping Midge would have more luck by tracking Greta down. JoAn Varner is the clubhouse manager. She kept the place in tip-top shape, but I found it hard to believe she'd know more than Rosemary about the community gossip or the residents' guests. Rosemary had handed my phone back to me and I switched to the next image in the queue. "One more question before we let you go. Have you ever seen him in here with this woman?" I asked.

"Whoa! That's the dead woman, isn't it? I knew I rec-ognized her when I caught a glimpse of her on *Dawn with Don & Deb*."

"That's our early morning local news show," Neely explained. "Not a reason to get up early, trust me." Rosemary shrugged.

"Not for you, maybe. I like their banter. Anyway, she's been in here, but not with that dreamboat in the picture on your phone or with Greta," Rosemary said. "You need to talk to Edgar Humphrey, our resident sugar daddy. She's only one of the young, attractive women he's had as companions over the years. From what I've heard," she added, lowering her voice, "he showers them with gifts until they move on."

"When they move on is it their idea or Edgar's?" I wondered aloud.

"You'll have to ask him. Maybe he gives them the boot when they start to get matrimony on their minds. He was engaged once, but that didn't work out well."

"What do you mean?"

"The woman sued him for palimony, even though he swore she never lived with him because of the age restriction issue." Another shrug told me we'd probably mined whatever information Rosemary had for us and we should get going since we still had lots more on our to-do list. Or maybe I wanted to leave because that the stupid age restriction issue had come up again and my guilty secret made me edgy. Neely said goodbye first, so I wasn't the only one ready to go.

"Under the right circumstances, Rosemary is a real hoot," Neely said once we were a few feet away from the reception desk. "She's very creative when it comes to setting up Cinema Circle events. You ought to check those out when you get a chance—especially if you like old movies. I still have a few connections from my years in show biz. Occasionally, I can get us a preview of an upcoming release, so it's not all vintage films. They always have an Oscar night party and Rosemary goes all out for it."

"I'd love to go with you the next time there's a film, old or new." I enjoy old movies. With the lights out, and a film running, there was little chance anyone could ask me personal questions about my husband.

"Let's find Chef Tony and see if he has anything to tell us," Neely said.

While we waited for Chef Tony, Neely and I canvassed the servers in the dining room. We had no luck getting any of them to identify the man caught spying on us the day before. One of the women we spoke to assured us she'd remember 'a hot guy like him' if he'd dined during one of her shifts. Her candid response made me believe that if he'd dined here, someone would have recalled his presence.

We also asked about Diana Durand. A couple of servers recognized "Dee," as they called the woman in our photo. They also confirmed that they'd seen her dining with a man. Like Rosemary, they claimed Dee was Edgar Humphrey's dining companion.

When Chef Tony joined us a few minutes later, he recognized the man immediately. He'd met him at the holiday brunch buffet pictured in the photo. My momentary excitement waned when Tony's recollections stalled out at that point. According to Tony, the guy's name might have been Dave or Dan. He couldn't be sure, but thought it was a simple man's name like that.

"Sorry, I can't be more help. He was nice and polite—loved the stuffing I served with the turkey. I don't recall ever seeing him the restaurant again with Greta or anyone else." Then he leaned in and whispered. "Does this have anything to do with the dead body you found? Is he a suspect?"

"I don't believe the police have any suspects yet—unless you've heard something we haven't," I replied. I was ready to leave at that point, but, fortunately, Neely decided to keep at it.

"How about this woman?"

"Oh, yeah, that's Dee somebody. She used to come in here with that lady killer, Edgar Humphrey." He turned and spoke directly to me.

"I don't know if you've been introduced to him. He's the debonair old gentleman who lives in the Twain cottage. When I heard he had a new love interest in his life, I wrote Dee off as another gold digger in a long line of cute young things after Edgar's money. When she stopped showing up with him, I figured he'd come to his senses and sent her on her way."

"Do you remember who told you that story about Edgar being involved with Dee?"

"Probably another Writers' Circle resident. Alyssa Gardener, maybe, or Robyn Chappell."

"Robyn's in the Shakespeare cottage," Neely said, figuring I hadn't met Robyn yet. "You can never tell where she comes up with the rumors she spreads. I've heard some doozies from her. She's not an owner, but rents the cottage. Robyn claims her landlord rented the cottage to her because it's haunted and the owner doesn't want to live in it anymore." Chef Tony responded with a shrug.

"I don't have that much contact with Robyn, so she hasn't told me that story. What I can tell you is that after Dee began coming in here on a regular basis with Edgar, her wardrobe improved considerably. The accessories, too.

She had a whopper of a diamond on her finger the last time I saw her. I remember it clearly, because I wondered if it meant she and Edgar were engaged. I hoped it wasn't true because I worried she'd help him on his way to the great beyond once they got married. Who knew she'd end up meeting her maker before Edgar?"

"Do you remember when you saw her wearing that ring?" I asked.

"It wasn't that long ago. Before I met you, so it's been a few months. You'd better ask Edgar." I nodded.

"We will. Thanks, Tony." Neely gave him a pat on his arm as we left the restaurant.

"No problem. I suppose I should quit referring to Edgar as a 'lady killer' shouldn't I? Under the circumstances, someone could get the wrong idea. At least until they take a good look at him." He didn't have to sell me on that idea. I had been introduced to Edgar Humphrey. A wraith of a man who prided himself on being a snappy dresser, he'd also bragged about his independence and the fact that he's the most senior resident in the Seaview Cottages community.

"Still living on my own, too, in the Twain Cottage. Not that I've learned much in almost a hundred years—'*I was young and foolish then; now I am old and foolisher.*'" He'd laughed when he quoted Mark Twain and that had sent him into a spasm of coughing. The middle-aged attendant with him at the time had intervened in a completely professional manner. I would never have guessed that "foolisher" part was true given his apparent preference for younger attendants who looked more like arm candy rather than skilled assistants.

"A sugar daddy would explain how Diana Durand had all those pricey goods with her at the time of her death," Neely commented. "Unless she's a secret heiress or something. I wonder if Charly's run a background check on her yet. She's a whiz with computers and has experience digging into a person's past." I gulped, wondering what Charly had dug up about me.

"Why is that?" I asked curious about Charly even though I realized, once again, how temperamentally unsuited I am to lead a life of deception. Before she could explain, Joe and Carl spotted us. They waved as Neely and I walked the short distance to the golf course maintenance garage that sits back a little behind the clubhouse.

"If you two are hoping to get in a round of golf, you're out of luck. The place is jumping today. Joe, here, was just about to suggest they rent the riding mowers."

"Whoever said there's no such thing as bad publicity had it right. Seaview Cottages is in the news as the possible site of a murder and we're booked solid. Can you believe it?" Joe asked.

"Yes, but they've got it wrong. The murder scene's not on our property."

"Fitzgerald's Bluff is close enough," Carl responded eying the two of us with curiosity or suspicion. "You two aren't interested in playing golf, are you?"

"No," I said. "We were hoping Joe might be able to tell us who rented a particular golf cart yesterday. Neely's got a photo of the tag on it."

"No problem. Hang on a second." Joe stepped through the open garage door into the service area. Off to the side was a computer sitting on a desk. He checked the number in that photo Neely's phone, hit a few keys, and looked up. "Greta Bishop reserved the cart for a foursome. They left here just after one and returned the cart at four-thirty. Does that do it for you?"

"All roads lead back to Greta, don't they?" Neely asked.

"They sure seem to when it comes to our mystery man," I agreed.

"Do you know if this guy was a member of the foursome?" She asked Joe.

"Yes. I've seen him with Greta before—one of those wheeler-dealer types she loves to hang around. Maybe another realtor or somebody in local politics or business. What difference does it make?"

"Yesterday afternoon he was in that cart alone and apparently trying to hang around with us." Neely gave the two men a quick rundown of what she meant by that. Carl shrugged.

"If he's one of Greta's business associates in real estate, it's not odd that he's checking the place out. You should track her down and ask what's up," Carl suggested as if we would never have come up with the idea to contact Greta. I'm sure he was trying to be helpful, so I smiled.

"When you find out what they're up to, fill me in, okay?" Joe asked. "Now I'm curious. I can ask around about him, too. If he's a big tipper or drops lots of money in the pro shop, they'll remember him. I might be able to get a name for you that way."

"Don't go to any trouble, but if you can do it in a casual way, that would be great. In the meantime, we're going to take Carl's advice and go straight to the source—

Greta Bishop." I walked out of the garage and onto the blacktop driveway area.

"It sounds like I need to keep this on the down low. Hush-hush. Top secret." Who knows how much longer he intended to go on like that. Neely cut him off by shoving her phone in front of him open to the picture of Diana Durand.

"Will you look at that?" Carl asked. "That's Edgar's woman friend, isn't it?"

"You're right! Girlfriend is more like it since she was young enough to be his daughter. Heck, that dude's so old, she could be his granddaughter or great-granddaughter for that matter."

"Not anymore," Neely said. "Diana Durand's dead."

"No way! It was her body on the bluff? The old coot's in trouble now. I warned him to stay away from her."

"He heard you. That's why they broke up," Carl retorted.

"If you knew he was involved in this mess, why didn't you tell us? It's only a matter of time before Deputy Devers figures it out!" Neely said, scolding them.

"Hey, don't blame me for not putting two and two together. I didn't see the body. I don't recognize her name, either. Does that name ring a bell for you, Carl?"

"No. Edgar called her Dee."

"He had a few other names for her too, when he'd had a drink or two." Joe smirked, raising both eyebrows a couple of times. I gave him a stern look and opened my mouth since I figured it was my turn to chew him out, but he stopped me.

"Save the dirty looks for Edgar. You and Deputy

Devers can double-team him—bad cop, bad cop."

"The deputy is even dumber than we think he is if he seriously believes Edgar had anything to do with her death. He would have been lying out there on the sand, too, if he'd tried to drag her body even a few inches. Before he got that new portable breathing thing he uses now, he huffed and puffed if he didn't have an assistant to haul his oxygen tank. That thing was on wheels."

"Not if he hired a hit man to do it for him. Edgar's loaded. He thinks it's hilarious when we call him a lady killer." Joe grinned. Neely and I both glared.

"Is that where Tony came up with the name?" I asked.

"Maybe. I could have gotten it from Tony or someone else. Edgar's not shy about the fact that he likes to walk around here with a foxy lady at his side. If he can get away with it, why not?" Joe's smile disappeared, and he shrank back a little as Neely and I continued to gaze at him in disapproval. "Uh, lady killer doesn't seem so funny now, does it?"

"No, it doesn't," I replied. Neely had more to say.

"You two jokesters are never as funny as you think you are. Don't go putting ideas into the deputy's head. His logical abilities are screwy enough without hearing your lady killer and hit man comments."

"You can quit worrying about us," Joe said. "The long arm of the law has already caught up with the old desperado. See?"

6

The County Hoosegow

NEELY AND I turned around to find Edgar wheeling his oxygen tank behind him, heading toward the entrance to the clubhouse. Deputy Devers was strutting on Edgar's right. A man in a sports jacket and jeans was on his left. Neely and I crossed the blacktop driveway in front of the maintenance garage to the parking lot outside the clubhouse. When Edgar saw us, he tipped the sporty hat he wore, and then spoke.

"Dee's dead. Darnell told the detective they call me a lady killer around here." Then he grinned. "I told them I didn't do it. These guys wanted to take me in for questioning. I told them that was fine if I could eat while they grill me. Grilled at the grill, get it?" That made Edgar laugh, which sent him into a coughing fit. The two men just stood there.

"You've got to be kidding!" I exclaimed. "Do you really believe this man strangled Diana Durand, dragged her body down to the beach, and hauled her far enough out into the water for it to carry her off?"

I didn't give them a chance to respond because Edgar was still coughing as if he couldn't get his breath back. I'd read somewhere that if a person who appears to be choking can speak, you can quit worrying about the need to intervene. Not that I knew what sort of intervention that might be in this case. Slapping him on the back seemed like it could send him sprawling.

"Are you okay, Edgar?" I asked. He gasped out a raspy reply.

"Yes." He breathed deeply from the contents of the tank he lugged with him. "I'm okay." He let go of the handle to the cart on which the tank was being wheeled, and I reached out to steady the tank before it could tumble to the ground. Neely lifted the deputy's hand that was dangling uselessly at his side and placed it on the handle of the cart.

"Deputy, you should be lugging that thing. Aren't you afraid a desperate killer like Edgar's going to pick it up and bash your brains in with it?" That set off another coughing spell as Edgar laughed again. Deputy Devers glowered, but he held onto the cart handle.

"I told the deputy he should wait for my assistant to show up," Edgar wheezed in between gulps of air from the tank. "He wanted to give me the third degree before I could run for it, I guess."

"Why are you using this decrepit tank thing? Where's the portable pack Midge ordered for you?"

"I dropped it in the hot tub. That's why Nancy's not here. She went to pick up another one for me. Then these guys showed up and I had to do something. Can you believe it still works?"

"No. Don't let Midge see you with it if you want to hang onto that antique," Neely warned him.

"Antique! That's a good one." Edgar slapped his knee at Neely's comment even though I'm sure she wasn't joking. Midge's nursing background might get the best of her if she spotted Edgar with the gear he had with him. Not an antique, but antiquated equipment in her mind I'm sure. I sighed, wondering once again how anyone could seriously consider Edgar as a suspect in Diana Durand's murder.

"You do know that lady killer thing's a joke, right?" I asked the deputy and the detective.

"Edgar's wanted for questioning in a murder investigation. I delivered him to the lead detective as requested. End of story."

"Deputy Do-wrong always gets his man, Edgar." Neely glowered at Devers. The man standing next to Devers suppressed a grin.

"At least the lead detective understands an old guy like me needs to eat lunch," Edgar said. "My last meal before they put me in the slammer."

The detective was an attractive man, especially when he smiled at Edgar's remark. He stared at Neely and me, perhaps wondering what we'd come up with next. I squirmed under his gaze, feeling a bit awkward about our outbursts. Still, what kind of a detective is he if he'd go after a fragile old man like Edgar Humphrey based on gossip from the deputy? As our eyes met, it's as if he read my mind.

"We're not here to arrest Mr. Humphrey. I prefer evidence to hearsay." Deputy Devers stiffened at that hearsay comment. "Besides, I'm inclined to believe him when he says he's a lover, not a killer, right Edgar?" Edgar just nodded, still taking deep breaths from the tank.

"We do have questions for Mr. Humphrey since he was acquainted with Diana Durand. For you, too, uh Ms.?"

"Webster—*Mrs.* Miriam Webster." I'm not sure why I felt compelled to add that "Mrs." to my name. There was something oddly disquieting and alluring in the directness of the detective's manner and the way in which he eyed me. With his pale blue eyes and salt and pepper hair, he reminded me of Paul Newman. Not the young Paul Newman, but an older version of the actor—somewhere in between his *Cool Hand Luke* and *Message in a Bottle* days. Where exactly, I couldn't say.

"I'm Cornelia Conrad, but everyone calls me Neely." Neely reached out and grasped the detective's outstretched hand. I followed her lead and did the same.

"I take it Deputy Devers is referring to you as the lead investigator on this case?" I asked.

"Yes. Detective Henry Miller at your service," he replied, smiling broadly, and still hanging onto my hand.

"Henry Miller, like the writer?" Neely asked. I pulled my hand away as she asked that question.

"Yes, although most people call me Hank."

"Nice to meet you, Hank," Joe said as he joined us. "Or should we call you Detective Miller?"

"Hank will do."

"I'm Joe Torrance and this is Carl Rodgers. We can vouch for Edgar if you need character references." The detective flipped a little notebook open and scanned what must have been notes.

"Yeah, he's a character—no doubt about it!" Carl

added. Neely and I glanced at each other, shaking our heads. Then we sent Carl our best, coordinated, "not funny" glares. The grin on Carl's face turned into a scowl.

"You two are listed as members of the party that stumbled on the body while it was still here, correct?"

"No, not us, Detective. That was Miriam. Well, Miriam and her dog, Domino," Carl replied.

"Miriam and Domino discovered the dead woman, but several others saw the body, too. By the time Joe, Carl, and I got to the crime scene, the body was gone. Didn't Deputy Devers fill you in on this? He must have told you about the loot we found there, even though the body had been moved."

"Of course, I did." Deputy Devers straightened up. There was little physical resemblance to Don Knotts, but something in the deputy's demeanor suddenly reminded me of Barney Fife. The annoying scrawny character on an old TV series starring Andy Griffith as a pleasantly folksy small-town sheriff, often swaggered his way into trouble the sheriff had to clear up. "You all shouldn't be too quick to take Edgar here off the hook. That ex-girlfriend of his called him the night she was killed."

"She did?" I asked. "Not from the dunes, though. You used your satellite phone, but we had to come back up here to the clubhouse because we couldn't get a decent signal down there."

"We don't know for sure what calls she made or when since we don't have her cell phone," Hank Miller admitted.

"Then what makes you think she called Edgar?" I asked.

"Jeanine Carlson, one of her coworkers told us she overheard Diana tell someone on the phone that she was going to call Edgar," the deputy explained in an annoyed tone.

"So? That doesn't mean she called him," Neely argued.

"Well the Carlson woman also told us Durand made another call and said 'Edgar, it's Dee.' I'm convinced."

"You can be as convinced as you want to be, Deputy. It doesn't matter one way or the other to me since I didn't speak to her anyway. If that's one of your questions, Detective, I can clear that up for you quickly. Can I go have lunch now?"

"Did she leave a message?" The detective asked.

"Maybe. I mostly use the real phone in my cottage. The red light wasn't blinking on the answering machine, so Dee didn't call me on that number. I don't have much luck picking up messages on the cell phone. Who has time to figure out all the voicemail and text messages or whatever else is on that thing?" Edgar dug into a pocket of the odd jacket he wore with madras golf pants.

"My kids insist I carry it with me in case I get into trouble. *'Help! I've fallen, and I can't get up.'*" Edgar whined in a high-pitched, nasal voice. "My daughter says it just like that! She's watched that silly commercial too many times. Here! Take the phone if you want it. Keep it! Now, if you guys want to ask me more questions, you've got to feed me." The detective took that phone from Edgar and examined it.

"Do I need a passcode to access your calls?" He asked.

"A what?" Edgar replied.

"I guess that's a no," Hank muttered as he slid Edgar's

phone into a pocket of his jacket.

"Please, Detective," I said. "What difference does it make if Diana called him or not? Do you believe Edgar dragged himself and his little cart out of his cottage, met her on the bluffs, and then killed her? One good whack with her Marc Jacobs tote bag and he would have been on the ground making that 'help I can't get up' call." I couldn't hide the exasperation from my voice.

"He could have done it if one of his geezer pals helped him," Deputy Devers offered before the detective could answer. The detective rolled his eyes at Devers' comment and my irritation toward Hank Miller fled.

"I've got this, Darnell. Mrs. Webster makes a valid point." Hank looked at me again with a good-natured expression on his face—even a twinkle in his eye.

"We just call her Miriam. There's no need to stand on formality around here Hank," Neely commented.

"You don't need to tell the Detective how to do his job," Devers said. "He's just trying to behave like a professional."

"How would you know?" Neely retorted. Detective Miller held up both hands.

"That's enough! I'm charging the next person who speaks with disturbing the peace. It's my peace your disturbing, but I'll make it stick long enough for one of you to cool your heels in the County hoosegow." I tried to keep from smiling, but the detective's use of that term hit my funny bone.

"Hoosegow?" I whispered before I could stop myself and then giggled. Neely snorted.

"Is that word even in the Merriam-Webster dictionary?" Joe asked. When I burst out laughing, it set off a round of guffaws. Devers smirked, but the rest of us roared with laughter—even the detective. Poor Edgar was sucking in big gulps of air from that tank again.

"Uh, do you want me to place her under arrest?" Devers asked. That set off another round of guffaws.

"No. Not until we give the folks at the hoosegow fair warning that Miriam Webster is on her way." The deputy did a double-take as if trying to figure out if the detective was serious.

"With her gang of old ladies, too. There's lots more where these came from." I laughed again when I realized he was serious!

"You'd better listen to the deputy, Detective. Forget about locking me up in the hoosegow because my posse will break me out of there in no time." Devers' mouth dropped open. He sputtered as we moved, en masse, toward the clubhouse entrance with Hank Miller leading the way.

"You do realize that breaking the law is no laughing matter, don't you?" Devers had both hands on his hips now that Edgar had taken back control of his cart. "Especially when we're in the middle of a murder investigation."

"Oh, lighten up, Devers," Neely said. "Haven't you noticed how skillfully the detective has rounded us all up for questioning? Let's have lunch and let him get the interviews done. Then, he can get back to the business of finding the strangler." Hank stopped and stared at Neely.

"I'm not grilling anyone because none of you are suspects. I'm not even taking formal statements since you didn't witness a crime either. I would like to hear the details about finding Diana Durand's body. I'd also like to know how you found out Diana Durand was strangled. We haven't released information yet about how she was killed."

"Midge Gaylord told us that after she examined the body," Neely replied.

"She's another of the old ladies I warned you about. An ancient Army nurse with an attitude," the deputy interjected.

I'll show you attitude, I thought, fighting off the urge to disturb the deputy's peace. Instead, I tried to explain what Midge had told us.

"Nothing that Deputy Devers just said matters except for the fact that Midge is a nurse. She recognized petechiae and other signs of strangulation on the victim." Hank nodded, acknowledging what I said as if I'd settled the matter.

"Let's keep it quiet for now, okay?" Hank asked. He got a round of yesses in response, from everyone except the deputy.

"Do you really believe these old codgers are going to keep their mouths shut about a woman being strangled?" Devers asked in a booming voice.

"Why don't we give you a megaphone and you can make sure everyone at Seaview Cottages hears you?" Neely asked. "He just said keep it quiet."

"Hank was speaking to you civilians, not to me."

"Well, I'm speaking to you, now, Darnell. If you can't keep your voice down, you can wait for me in the patrol car." The deputy's mouth opened but he kept quiet. "Let's not get ahead of ourselves by characterizing Edgar or anyone else as a suspect either."

"It's okay, Detective. I've got an alibi. My nephew, Howard, spent the night at my place as he often does," Edgar said. "I didn't do it and I doubt anyone else here at Seaview Cottages did it either."

"Unless it was the guy in the golf cart Miriam and Neely caught spying on the Writers' Circle cottages yesterday."

"What?" Hank asked Joe.

"I can explain. I'll show you his picture too if it will help."

"Don't bother, Miriam. I'm sure the detective has his eye on the men Dee was dating after we broke up. She called me about a month ago asking for money. Dee didn't bring it up, but I heard later that at least one of the men in her life was giving her trouble."

"What men?" Neely, the detective, and I asked, almost in unison.

7

Money or Men?

"**H**OW MUCH MONEY?" Carl asked. He would zero in on the money angle given that he was the manager of a collection agency before he retired. I was curious about how much money Diana wanted Edgar to give her, too.

"Hang on, Edgar before you answer Carl's question about money or ours about the men, okay? I'm going to ask if we can have lunch in a private dining room if there's one available." He nodded.

When we'd walked into the clubhouse, I was suddenly aware of how conspicuous we were, even if we kept our voices down. Half a dozen people were in the lobby and they all turned to stare at us as we headed to the seating station in the Dunes Club.

Why not? Deputy Devers was with us. He stands out in his uniform and in most peoples' memories. Midge and her pals aren't the only ones who have nicknames for him. Soon after I arrived in the community, Midge brought me to lunch here. Someone had wiped away "Chef's Specialty of the Day" on the blackboard. Instead it read, "Deputy's Special Name of the Day."

Diners had exhibited lots of creativity on the board that day. I wondered how much Hank Miller knew about his sidekick. When I stole a glance at the detective, he was watching me.

"Good grief," I whispered to myself.

"What is it?" Neely asked.

"I know the detective said we're not suspects, but he's looking at me like I'm in a police lineup. Maybe he's having second thoughts since no one else was with us when Domino and I found the body."

"Honey, you have been married a long time, haven't you? He's checking you out. That's what men do when they meet an interesting, attractive woman. Relax—as much as you can under the circumstances. He's got a nice smile, doesn't he?"

"I guess so." To be honest, I had noticed his smile. Those blue eyes, too. I wasn't going to admit it and sound like a married woman with a roving eye. "I'll give him credit for managing the deputy well. How awful must it be to have to spend the whole day with Devers?"

"Like a lower level in *Dante's Inferno*," Neely quipped. "Hank Miller's a saint."

Just then Chef Tony appeared. His good humor was an instant antidote to the miserable deputy's nastiness. Tony had worked in high-end hotels much of his life. He'd even had his fifteen minutes of fame as a personal chef to a Hollywood hottie who turned out to be a flash in the pan.

Even though I haven't known him long, Tony strikes me as a happy, humble man with a great sense of humor. The kind of man to whom I believed I was married. A year after his death, I'm not so sure who Peter Webster really was behind his happy-go-lucky, "can-do" veneer.

"Come on, Miriam. Let me escort you and your dining companions to the Par 3 room." As soon as we were seated, servers handed out menus, took our beverage orders, and left. Then Tony filled us in on the daily specials.

"I highly recommend today's special—bowtie pasta with artichoke hearts and chicken in a vinaigrette marinade. It's served with a small salad or the soup of the day, which is a smoky roasted corn chowder. Shoo Fly Pie for dessert." Chef Tony gave me a little smile.

"That's one of Miriam's recipes, I'll bet. I've never heard of it being served around here," Carl suggested.

"Yes. She tells me it's a favorite among the Amish in Ohio and the Pennsylvania Dutch. After a slice of that pie served warm with a scoop of vanilla ice cream, you'll know why."

"Ohio or Pennsylvania?" The detective asked. Hank was staring at me again in a way that made me squirm. The personal questions did, too. I tried to sound nonchalant and to keep my response light-hearted.

"Ohio. I used to work in the business office at a bakery before I retired. It seems like a crime to let all their delicious recipes go to waste. I share them whenever I can."

"Miriam's your prime suspect if chocolate ever turns out to be the cause of death." Neely went on to tell them about the chocolate cake we'd eaten at dinner the night before. Tony asked for the recipe, which I promised to send him, and then left. The moment he was gone, Neely returned to the discussion about why Death by Chocolate

Cake had been such an apt dessert last night.

"We needed the cake after the day we had. A strangler and a stalker on the same day." Then she passed her phone to the detective and showed him the photo of the man on the golf cart. "So far, we haven't figured out who he is, but our friend, Midge, is working on it. If you scroll to the next picture, you can see he's not a stranger. In the second photo, he's with Greta Bishop at a holiday party." Deputy Devers took a cursory look at the man riding in the golf cart as the photo passed. Then he shrugged.

"He doesn't look like a stalker to me."

"Okay, maybe stalker is too strong a word. Let's say he's just being a nosy parker or he's an overly exuberant looky-loo. I don't care. Miriam says he took off in a hurry when Domino barked at him. Why would he do that if he wasn't up to something shady?"

"Maybe he doesn't like dogs. Especially big, noisy ones with spots all over them." The deputy scowled as if he had a bad taste in his mouth. I felt like growling like a dog.

"That's ridiculous! Who wouldn't like Domino?" Neely asked.

The detective had glanced at the photo of our visitor in the golf cart, then flipped to the next photo, and peered at it. Edgar, who'd been chomping on a breadstick, swallowed, and then leaned over to check out the picture, too. He waved a half-eaten breadstick at the photo as he spoke.

"That's Dave Winick. Dee introduced him to me at the dinner. He's a hotshot at the Blue Haven Resort. I figured Greta Bishop had designs on him by the way she was making a fool of herself. Maybe he has designs on Seaview Cottages and that's why he was on the prowl yesterday."

Then we all shut up again as the servers returned with our soups and salads. They topped off our beverages and then left us alone. The door had barely shut when Deputy Devers fired a question that he must have been chomping at the bit to ask.

"Why would a hotshot with the Blue Haven Resort have any interest in this place?"

"Geez, Darnell, for most people that wouldn't be a difficult question to answer. It's not called *Seaview* Cottages for no reason. This is prime real estate even if someone bought the property, tore everything down, and started over." It was Carl's turn to wave a breadstick— aiming it at the smirking deputy.

"Oh, man, don't say that! Nobody's getting near the Chandler cottage after the upgrades I've put into it. The golf course is in primo condition now, too."

"Since Dave Winick was in a golf cart, is it wrong to assume he'd been out on the course?" Hank asked.

"No," I said. "Joe didn't have his name, but he told us he recognized him as part of a foursome with Greta Bishop. They headed out onto the course early in the afternoon. We're concerned that it's a little too much of a coincidence that he was skulking around our cottages the same day we found Diana Durand's body nearby on Fitzgerald's Bluff. I'm not sure how much the deputy told you about the timing of events, but we believe there's a good chance whoever killed Diana moved the body soon after we left to call the police."

"So?" Devers asked.

"*So*, Darnell, they're worried the killer was still around, got a look at them, and is after them, now." I nodded as the detective said that. Stated in such a matter of fact way, it sounded foolish to me, but not to Neely.

"Exactly!" She exclaimed. "Although, I'm not sure why a ruthless killer crafty enough to go back and get rid of the body, would be so obvious about tracking us down."

"He wasn't that crafty, or the body would have disappeared completely," Carl asserted. "Even though Edgar's made it clear Dave Winick knew Dee, it's hard to imagine he's the culprit. If what Edgar says about his bigwig status with Blue Haven is true, he must be a smart guy. I don't like coincidences, but I doubt he was taking pictures of your cottages because he's got murder on his mind."

"Smart guys can be too smug for their own good, and bigwigs too big for their britches," Edgar said.

"Is that a quote from Mark Twain?" Joe asked.

"Nope. That's all me."

"I don't get it. What makes you so sure the killer was still around?" Devers asked. I bit my lip and resisted the impulse to chew the deputy out for not being more concerned about what had happened yesterday. It probably wouldn't have mattered anyway given how oblivious he still was to the implications of the issues we'd raised. Instead of grousing, I went through the sequence of events as they'd unfolded the day before. Neely helped me estimate the time at points along the way.

"That's a tight timeframe, Detective," Neely said once I'd finished the rundown. "The killer couldn't have been too far away to be able to get rid of the body before we all showed up again with Devers." Hank nodded.

"Domino seems like a great dog. Did he…"

"She," I said, correcting the detective.

"Did she do anything to suggest someone was nearby when she found the body?" A little shiver ran through me as I recalled events—including an incident I'd overlooked.

"I didn't realize it at the time, but when she barked frantically, I did notice something. Her barking is what drew Midge and the women out walking with her to us. I assumed Domino had heard them higher up on the trail and that's what set her off. Or she was just agitated, sensing my shocked reaction to the body she'd found."

"Did you hear or see anything else before the women arrived?"

"No, but I did catch a hint of a fragrance. I figured it had come from perfume the dead woman was wearing. Now that I think about, though, it was on the breeze coming from behind me." That shiver returned.

"Maybe one of the walkers wore it."

"No, Deputy. If that were true, I wouldn't be bringing it up now," I snapped, as the urge to growl at him returned.

"Marty's allergic to heavy fragrances," Neely explained. "I'm talking about Marty Monroe, Detective. She must be on the list of names Devers gave you." Hank scanned the list and nodded. Then Neely continued. "Her allergies were one reason she retired as a buyer. She got to the point that she couldn't handle all the odors coming from cosmetic counters in department stores. We never wear anything like that around her. It's no big deal for me anyway. I didn't pick up the habit of wearing perfume, even though I worked with lots of people who promoted fragrances as well as cosmetics when I was a makeup artist."

"I'm glad to hear that, Neely. I can't stand the stuff now that my lungs don't work as well as they did. Dee quit wearing it around me too. Maybe she picked up the habit again after we quit seeing each other, but I think you're on to something, Miriam. Dave Winick was wearing an after shave or cologne or something smelly when I met him. Maybe it was him hiding out there behind you on the bluff."

"Could Dave Winick have been one of the men Diana was dating after you broke up with her?"

"I don't know. When I asked about him, Dee told me he was 'an old short-burning flame.' By the way he responded to Greta's flirting, I took Dee's word for it and bought her story. Remember, I'm an old fool, though, so who knows?"

"You said 'men,' Edgar. I take it there was more than one man in Diana Durand's life after you?" Edgar nodded in response to the detective's question. Before he could speak, the servers were back with our meals. When the door closed behind, them Joe added his two cents' worth to the conversation.

"It'd take more than one man to make up for Edgar, wouldn't it?" Joe asked and then dug into the enormous burger they'd brought him.

"Yep. I've seen her around town several times with different men. She seemed happy as a clam from what I could tell. Alf and Alyssa told me they saw Dee with some guy, though, when that wasn't the case. They were in the parking lot near a restaurant at the Blue Haven Resort. You know, the one with ocean views."

"He means The Oceano Room," Joe explained. "It's

pricey and the food isn't any better than Tony's."

"I won't disagree with you about Tony's cooking. Anyway, that's the place where Alf and Alyssa Gardener told me they saw her arguing with a man. Then, he grabbed her by the arm and she slapped him. She stormed off, got into her car, and tore out of there, or they would have called the police."

"Wow! Edgar's right that you should be checking out her new boyfriends. If they got into a physical fight in public, an argument could have been much worse if it happened out on the bluffs alone late at night or early in the morning," Carl said.

"Who was he?" I asked.

"They didn't give me a name, but they said he was a big guy with almost no hair. Rough-looking. He had a scar on his cheek and a wrecked ear that sounded to me like what you'd see on a boxer or street fighter, maybe."

"Okay, so that's definitely not Dave Winnick," I muttered, feeling relief and disappointment at the same time. I realized how much I hoped we'd bring closure to this mess in a hurry. I'd ditched our usual walk to the beach and stayed in the Writers' Circle neighborhood this morning when I took Domino out for her walk. Even that had felt uncomfortable thanks to Dave Winick's unwelcome visit.

"Did they hear what the argument was about?" Hank asked.

"Money."

"How much did he want? Maybe she borrowed money from the wrong people and the guy was in a more disreputable side of the collection business," Carl suggested.

"She was demanding money, not him, if Alf and Alyssa

heard it right. You'd better ask them. My memory isn't as good as it used to be, and I wasn't that interested in Dee's problems with money or men. Maybe that was a mistake given what's happened to her."

"Was that before or after Diana Durand asked you for money?" Carl piped up again.

"After. The argument in the parking lot was recent."

"Carl asked this question already, but I'm curious too. How much money did she want from you, Edgar?" Hank asked.

"A few thousand—just to tide her over until she got a check—a tax refund or a bonus, or something like that." We'd met Edgar's response about a few thousand dollars with a round of gasps. Not Hank Miller, though, whose curiosity had moved on to another interesting matter.

"Did you give it to her?" He asked.

"No. I told her to sell that diamond friendship ring I'd given her. She might have had to drive to Santa Barbara or LA to sell it, but it would have given her the money she asked for and then some."

"Whoa, Edgar, you're lucky you're not the one who turned up dead," Joe said. "It's a good thing you told Dee no over the phone. In person, she might have decked you if she'd slapped you the way she did the big guy." Joe shook his head as he went back to eating.

"A few thousand sounds like more than 'tide her over' money," Carl observed. "In my experience, people who dig that kind of a hole for themselves are often addicted to something—gambling or drugs."

"Shopping, maybe, if she got accustomed to living at the level Edgar's generosity afforded her," I suggested recalling the load of merchandise lying on the ground near where we'd seen her body.

"She did love shopping. I didn't mind, and it didn't bother me that she got used to my generosity, either. What ended our friendship was the pressure she put on me to tie the knot. I may be a fool, but I'm not that big a fool. I've got better uses for my money than to turn a woman like Diana Durand into the merry widow."

"I'm surprised she took no for an answer if she needed money that bad. Some of the deadbeats I've run into have hit up their relatives and friends relentlessly until they gave them more money just to make them go away," Carl said.

"Until the next time, right?" Hank asked. Carl nodded.

"She didn't keep badgering me," Edgar commented, "but before she gave up, Dee did make another ridiculous attempt to get money by offering to sell me information about some deal she thought I should know about."

"What kind of a deal?" Hank asked.

"Who knows? I was so fed up at that point I told her I wasn't interested. Period. I've never liked to mix business and pleasure, even back when I gave a hoot about business. Anyway, I chalked it up to another childish effort to pull the wool over my eyes by trying to make herself out as a woman of intrigue or a wheeler-dealer. She was very immature, which is another reason I ended the relationship."

"Geez, Edgar, what did you expect from a twenty-something woman willing to play you as her sugar daddy?" Joe asked. Edgar shrugged. I could tell Hank was still mulling over Edgar's revelations. I was too.

"Okay, so is it money or men?" I wondered aloud.

"That is an excellent question," Hank replied. "Love and money are two of the oldest motives in the book for murder. Maybe the crime scene investigators will turn up evidence that leads back to a suspect or reveals a motive. You never know where the lead you need will turn up."

"You all will lay off and give the authorities time to figure this out, if you know what's good for you," the deputy warned. I'm sure he intended that to be an order. I resisted the urge to salute, which wasn't too hard since he issued the command by pointing a fork at us before shoveling more food into to his mouth. There was something almost comical in his behavior.

"I hope you've left room for dessert, Deputy." I smiled, feeling a little sheepish knowing we wouldn't heed that warning no matter how solemnly he'd delivered the message.

"No way am I going to miss an opportunity to try Shoo Fly Pie that comes with a recommendation from a guy who can cook like Tony. This community isn't all bad," Devers commented.

Hank didn't acknowledge the deputy's remark with a verbal reply. Instead, he smiled at me, rolled his eyes, heavenward, and shook his head. I couldn't help responding returning the smile.

Hank does inspire more confidence than Deputy Dolittle, I thought, wondering if I'd just come up with a new moniker for Hank's irritating sidekick.

We'd lapsed into a few minutes of silence to do some serious eating when the detective went on alert. Finished with his meal, Hank had been scrolling through the calls on Edgar's phone.

"Well, well, Edgar, Diana did call you. You've got a missed call from her at around the time the Carlson woman claimed she called you. Here's a new twist, though. You've got another missed call from her placed after she was dead."

"Don't tell me she called to ask for money from the other side?" He asked. That set off a round of nervous laughter as the servers swept into the room with pie and ice cream, "compliments of the Chef."

8

Rivals 'Til the End?

NEELY AND I had just left the clubhouse when she repeated the question I'd asked earlier. "What's your guess—is it money or men?"

"I don't know. Let's check with Midge and see if she learned anything more about Dave Winick or what he's doing roaming around here on his own. Maybe he's house-hunting on behalf of real-estate hungry developers at Blue Haven and that's the deal Diana wanted to share with Edgar—for a price."

"I considered that, which would make this about money. It's also possible Dave wasn't happy about being relegated to the status of an old flame. Diana wouldn't be the first woman to be killed after an affair ended—especially if it was her idea to call it quits and not his. Winick could be one of those guys who can't take no for an answer. There must be some gossip about their break up since they both worked for 'Big Blue' at the time."

"'Big Blue,' huh? That's new."

Neely stopped for a second to take in the views of the Pacific Ocean that were visible along the walking path to our Writers' Circle cottages. It was a dazzling sight with the scruffy, rolling bluffs and sandy dunes sprawled out below the Seaview Cottages community. The breeze ruffled patches of scruffy grass and a pair of gulls overhead called out. In the distance, children screeched as if echoing the gulls' cries.

"It's not just the people who have nicknames around here. We're nickname crazy, I guess, with names for bluffs and dunes, coves and beaches. You know about Fitzgerald's Bluff, of course. That hillock is Dickens' Dune," she said pointing into the distance. "We call that small inlet, Steinbeck's Cove. Why not have a nickname for the resort, too? In this case, I'm almost positive it's a name the workers at the resort came up with and not one of Midge's creations." Neely began walking again, picking up the pace as we headed into the enclave in which our homes are located.

"Diana sure had her share of trouble there. Not just the big guy in the parking lot, but the unfriendly coworker who's willing to smear her in the media, and an affair with a bigwig that may or may not have ended well. Blue Haven was no haven with Diana around, was it?" I asked.

"Nope. Let's see what Marty found out if she was able to reach her old friend today as she planned. Do we have any of that cake left?"

"Yes. I was thinking about taking it to Rosemary this afternoon and having her offer it to folks who drop by the clubhouse. I'm going to blow up like a Macy's Day Parade balloon if I don't cool it."

"Let your posse of old ladies rescue you from the leftover cake. Dinner's at my house tonight—sixish. I'll just make a big Greek salad with feta cheese and Kalamata olives. If we eat a light meal, you'll feel less guilty about scarfing down another piece of that decadent cake. As you can probably tell by looking at me, I have no problem carrying a few extra pounds." Neely laughed in her characteristic rich, hearty way. She pushed her glasses up on her nose and looked at me, her dark eyes glinting.

"Then, we'll get down to business. We have plenty of news to share from lunch with our engaging new detective friend. What a pleasant change he is after wrestling with Devers for years." I had to agree with her given how soon I'd come up with my own derogatory name for the deputy.

"Hank has a knack for calling the deputy by his first name in a way that stings as much as one of Midge's fake names for Darnell." I tried my best to emulate the detective's emphasis and intonation when I said Darnell.

"That's close, but you need to hear the detective say it a few more times to mimic him properly." She raised her eyebrows a couple times. "I'm sure he won't mind." I tried not to blush. Maybe, because I suddenly realized I hoped she was right that Hank wouldn't mind seeing me again.

When we arrived minutes later at my cottage, Neely waved at Domino who was peering out of the picture window that overlooks the porch. My sweet spotty dog's tail was swinging wildly. I heard muted woofs coming from inside the house.

"Why not bring your lovely girl with you? I'm sure Charly will bring Emily and the two dogs can keep each other company."

"That would be wonderful. Domino has settled in pretty well, but I don't like leaving her home alone too much." Our move to the West Coast wasn't the first adjustment

Domino had been forced to make. For the first few weeks after Pete died, she continued to wait for him to come home at dinner time each evening. Then, she'd park herself near the chair he sat in after dinner to watch TV.

I tried to fill in for him by sitting in that chair. Or maybe I had filled that empty seat for myself. When I sold the house and moved a few months later, I got rid of the chair along with tons of other stuff. Domino and I went from a house that had become too big for just the two of us, to a tiny apartment that had us almost stumbling over each other. As I walked in through the front door of my Hemingway Cottage, I was struck once again by the "just right" feeling it evoked.

"Hello, Domino, you good dog! Goldilocks is home." Domino woofed in reply. "Do you want to visit Emily tonight?" I asked. You don't have to ask Domino twice about going to a party. She spun around and then leaped in the air—a near-perfect imitation of Emily's Jack Russell Terrier antics.

What a memory she has, I thought. "It's too bad you didn't catch a glimpse of Diana Durand's killer. I bet you could help us find that person, couldn't you?"

When I recalled how Domino had darted toward Dave Winick, I put him back on the list of suspects. It could be she just didn't like an unfamiliar person poking around. On the other hand, maybe she sensed—or smelled something that had set her off. I suddenly had an idea that might help sort things out.

"I wonder what cologne Dave Winick wears, Domino." She cocked her head to one side as I spoke. I'd started talking to my pets long before I'd become a widow, but it's a regular occurrence now. "It's a familiar fragrance. Maybe they sell it at one of the Blue Haven Resort shops. We might at least be able to figure out if it's a fragrance sold to men or women." When she tilted her head the other way, I laughed. The best part about having a fur baby like my Domino, besides the scintillating conversation, is that she makes me laugh out loud every day.

"You're such an inspiration! It's time for members of our gang of old ladies to go undercover as mystery shoppers—pun intended. Come on, I'll get you a treat!"

I felt incredibly antsy as I did a few chores. I kept going over and over what we'd learned from our conversations with people today. As I did that, I also tried not to linger too long on Hank's face, his laugh, or his comments. That wasn't easy.

"Focus, Miriam!" I said sharply, speaking to myself out loud. Domino's head popped up.

"It's okay, sweetie. I'm just driving myself nutty—nuttier—wondering how we're going to figure this out." Domino wagged her tail in what I regarded as a sympathetic, understanding way. She'd had lots of practice doing that since Pete died. "At least snooping into murder and mayhem will keep me from stewing about Pete and all the lies I'm hanging onto. They're not all so little, though, are they?" Some of Pete's secrets had been big ones. I tried never to call them lies, but that was harder to do now that I was haunted by my own deception.

My gut told me we'd learn something by making the rounds at the Blue Haven Resort, even if we couldn't track down that fragrance I'd encountered out among the dunes.

I made a cup of tea and sat down at the dining table in the kitchen. I spent the next hour checking out the resort website. As distasteful as I found the task, I went over the Seaview Cottages financial situation again. Then I read through the news coverage about Diana's murder and came face-to-face, once again, with Hank Miller.

"Good grief! You're a married woman as far as your friends and neighbors are concerned," I muttered, sighing as I closed the lid on my laptop. "Despite my wandering eye, Domino, I assure you that may not have been a completely fruitless effort. Maybe it is about the money after all. Let's go see what our Writers' Circle friends have to say about what I found!" Domino jumped up and wiggled toward me. "Go" is a word she knows and loves!

Whenever I'm invited to someone's home for dinner or a party, I try to give them a few extra minutes before I show up. That's not out of a desire to be fashionably late, but an effort to be polite. I'm one of those people who always have last-minute things to do when I've invited people over, and I run around like a crazy woman until the last second. Despite being "politely late" when I arrived for the chili supper at Charly's house last night, I'd still been her first guest. Not tonight. By the time Domino and I showed up, the others were already there.

"Hello, everyone! You all must be excited to share what we've learned about the body on the bluff," I said when Neely led me to the dining area where the others were gathered around a platter of hummus and pita bread triangles.

"Nah, we can hardly wait for another piece of your Death by Chocolate Cake!" Marty quipped.

"Yep!" Neely said as she whisked that cake out of my hands. Charly removed Domino's leash and turned her loose with Emily in Neely's backyard. The fence around Neely's yard was a brilliant white color like mine, but taller and appeared to be in much better shape. A taller, sturdier fence was appealing. My cottage hadn't been built on a lot with as high an elevation as the Christie Cottage, so I'd lose my view of the golf course. Under the current circumstances, it might be worth it. At least Emily and Domino could romp without worrying that they'd get out or an unwelcome guest could get in.

"Let's eat!" Neely announced moments later. "We can wait until we finish dinner if you'd like or we can dig into our food and our crime at the same time."

"Well, I'll save my news from the preliminary autopsy report until after dinner. It's not very appetizing. Why don't you and Miriam fill us in on your lunch meeting? Hank Miller won't spoil our appetite. He's not only a competent detective, but easy on the eyes, isn't he?" Charly glanced from Neely to me and then settled back on Neely waiting for a reply. Instead of answers, she got more questions.

"He is?" Marty asked.

"How do you know?" Midge asked. "Was he one of your students?"

"He went through the Police Academy before I started teaching courses for them, but I've met him. He's a friend of a friend."

"I didn't know you taught at the Police Academy," I said glad to learn a little more about Charly's background.

"That was after she retired. Dr. Penelope aka 'Charly'

Parker was a criminology professor at UC Santa Cruz," Neely said. "As obsessed as she is about all things related to the Brontë sisters, I assumed she was a professor of literature or creative writing until I heard otherwise."

"Not just a sit behind the desk kind of a professor, either," Midge added. "She helped solve the murder of a colleague while she was at the university and consulted on several other crimes as well."

"Like a profiler?" I asked.

"Something like that, but more sociological than psychological," Charly replied. "There's lots of social data that can be helpful in figuring who's a likely culprit. Group data's not always that great at picking out an individual, but it can often narrow down the list of suspects. Especially when you link it with an individual's personal history and past behavior. A sociological bias can also get in your way when it comes to finding a killer. It's been years since I was involved with law enforcement as a consultant. It still irks me to see a guy like Devers throwing his weight around as if his job is about wielding power rather than seeking justice."

"At least he's mostly assigned to patrolling the highways, dealing with fender benders, and traffic problems," Marty offered.

"True, and it's good he doesn't have much of a role to play in this investigation. Devers has already demonstrated what a hard time he has recognizing evidence of a crime," Charly added.

"Even with a gang of old ladies pointing right at it." With that, Neely launched into her account of our lunch meeting. Everyone laughed when she explained how I'd warned them that the gang of old ladies Devers bad-mouthed would break me out of the hoosegow.

When Neely and I finished giving everyone an overview of our lunch discussion, Midge zeroed in on Dave Winick. During her conversation with Greta Bishop, she'd also discovered our golf cart stalker's name. She'd learned more about him and his relationships with Greta and Diana.

"It's interesting that Edgar claims Diana Durand's relationship with Dave Winick was old news. Greta said she got 'hands off' vibes from her. A nasty comment went with Greta's claim. 'Some women just can't handle it when a man moves on.' Something catty like that."

"I'll bet it wasn't the only snide comment she made about Diana, was it?" Charly asked Midge.

"No. It's not worth repeating. Greta made it clear she didn't like Diana. There's also no doubt in my mind that Greta's got something going on with Dave Winick. Her dislike for Diana could be about a rivalry over Dave."

"Okay, so our question raised at lunch still stands. Was Diana's murder about money or men? Is Dave Winick a boy toy, the love of her life, or what?" Neely asked. "She denied being able to lug Diana's dead body into the water, but did she appear to be angry enough to want her dead?"

9

Money *and* Men

"I DON'T KNOW. Maybe it's about money *and* men. Greta's got a cougar side, but she's also a business-woman. She made a point of telling me how 'connected' Dave is, and what 'an asset' he is as a business associate. When I asked what kind of an asset he was, she played coy at first, but then told me not to be so naïve. 'No one gets a deal done around here unless they're in tight with the powers that be at Big Blue.' My hunch is the predator in her is more interested in making a killer deal than a romantic conquest."

"Cougars have big, sharp claws," Neely said. "If Diana got in the way of the man and the deal—look out!"

"My mind raced along the same track," Midge responded. "Greta must have sensed it and cut straight to the chase. 'In case you're imagining I had anything to do with Diana Durand's death, forget it. My bad back wouldn't let me haul that cow down to the water even if I'd been angry enough to kill her. I'm old, remember?'" Midge spoke Greta's words using a huffy tone that fit Greta to a T.

"Wow! The word is out about how Diana ended up at

Blue Haven, isn't it?" I asked.

"Around here, anyway. I told you this place thrives on gossip, especially if motor mouths like Alyssa Gardener and Greta Bishop are in on it. Rosemary does a pretty good job of circulating hot news, too," Charly commented.

"Did Greta say anything about why Dave was taking pictures of our cottages?" I asked.

"Greta claimed she was in a hurry when they finished their golf game and he offered to return the cart. In her words, 'So what if he looked around on his way to the cart drop 0ff?' She didn't seem surprised or creeped out about his surveillance the way we were. Maybe Deputy Devers isn't the only one hoping our community will go into receivership."

"A vulture waiting to pick over the bones of our dead community instead of a Peeping Tom or a strangler, huh?" Neely asked.

"That's still creepy," Marty added.

"It could be dead on, though." Then I realized what I'd said. "Sorry, that wasn't the best choice of words under the circumstances, was it?" I paused and started over.

"What I'm trying to say is that I found an interesting news item about 'Big Blue' that buzzed around on social media. Apparently, it's no secret that 'Big Blue' aims to become even bigger. They want to open timeshares and expand into vacation condos and residential property."

"That's not a surprise," Midge said. "They've been squawking about that for years. There was lots of excitement about it until real estate prices tumbled."

"Well, what caught my eye was a mention by a local

blogger that we're in the 'path of progress' and slated to become Blue Haven Seaview Cottages. The corporate office trounced the idea, publicly, but I also went through the minutes of the Financial Committee's meetings. About six months ago, someone floated the idea to the committee members and riled everyone up because it was a real lowball offer. I don't see any formal paperwork on file, so the discussion must have occurred off the record."

"Greta didn't say a word about it. I was more interested in the reason she was ogling Dave Winnick in that photo, so I didn't press her about business deals with the guy. The discussion was closed so fast it doesn't matter much anyway, does it?"

"I don't even remember hearing a word about it. Not even through the rumor mill around here," Charly added. "That doesn't mean whoever wanted to make a deal has given up. If it was Dave Winick or someone else at Blue Haven, Diana could have caught wind of it and that's what she thought Edgar would be willing buy from her."

"Whatever information Diana wanted to sell to Edgar, I doubt she got it in a legit way, don't you?" Neely asked.

"No matter how she got her hands on secret or sensitive information, someone might have objected to her offering to sell it. Her sugar daddy may not have been the only person she approached with information to peddle," I suggested.

"That could have been asking for trouble," Midge added. "If word got out earlier than the dealmakers wanted, it could have raised enough interest to create a little competition and drive the price up."

"Or given us time to mobilize to protect our property,

depending on what kind of angle Winick and his pals were working on," Neely added. "They must have something tricky up their sleeves to be at it again. I wish Edgar had been a little more curious about her offer. We don't even know for sure that's what she was peddling to him."

"None of that seems worth killing her over, does it?" I asked.

"It does if the angle Winick was working was an illegal one. He doesn't strike me as the kind of man who'd go to jail without putting up a fight."

"From what my friend, Donna Wolz, told me, getting herself mixed up in all sorts of trouble wasn't anything new. Rumor has it that Diana left the Bay Area when her agent's wife found out he was managing more than her musical career."

"Some people can't learn, can they? Having an affair with Dave Winick is almost as dumb as taking up with a married man. It wasn't smart on his part either, although the more junior member of a duo like that usually ends up with the short end of the stick when the music stops."

Charly sure had that part right. The Pastry Palace was a large enterprise before the Great Recession tanked it. A surprising amount of hanky-panky went on over the years, much of it involving an errant nephew of the company's founder. The nephew stayed put, but the women with whom he'd become involved moved on—one way or another.

"To make matters worse, Diana blabbed about her affairs. That didn't go over well with her coworkers. No one wanted to say a bad word about their jobs or the company when a colleague might intentionally or accidentally share it with one of the bosses as 'pillow talk.'"

"Edgar said there was more than one man in her life after they broke up. Did your friend come up with any other names?" Neely asked.

"Most of Donna's information comes from the shop managers, not the staff. The managers all know Dave Winick by sight and by name given his prominence as Director of Development for Blue Haven Resort Properties. Donna didn't mention any other men by name. The manager of the shop where Diana worked complained about the antagonism Diana stirred up. Diana was undependable—showed up late and missed shifts altogether. That upset her coworkers who had to cover for her. Especially when Dave paid Diana's supervisor a visit and told her to lighten up after she took Diana to task and wrote her up for missing her shift without calling in."

"Why am I not surprised? That explains why she didn't get fired," Midge commented.

"That guy has big time, boundary issues—maybe even legal boundaries," Charly said, shaking her head. "Dumb, too. Not only does he get romantically involved with a subordinate, but then intervenes on her behalf. That's a recipe for disaster if love turns into loathing. Diana could have used that if she'd decided to file charges against him for sexual harassment."

"That's an interesting idea. Diana needed money, maybe she was threatening to charge Winick or to report their affair to his bosses unless he paid her off," Neely suggested.

"Or maybe that's the information she wanted to sell to Edgar. If Big Blue's planning to make a grab for our cottages, a sexual harassment scandal involving a top exec might slow things down. It could even kill the deal if it instigated enough trouble for the partners to lose confidence in each other. Maybe she thought Edgar would be willing to pay to be able to stop having his home sold out from under him."

"I hear you, Midge," Charly said, shrugging. "At this point, Neely's right that we don't have any proof there's a deal in the works. And we don't even know if Diana Durand and Dave Winick had a bad break up that might have angered her enough to turn on him. Apparently, she didn't fling a drink on him or act out when he showed up at that holiday dinner with Greta Bishop."

"That's true," I said. "Did your friend say anything about if and when the affair between Durand and Winick ended?"

"No. Either she didn't have the details, or she wasn't willing to share them with me. Donna did give me the name of the person she believes was the anonymous coworker who had nasty things to say to the press about Diana." Marty paused to check what must have been a note she made on her phone. "Her name is Andrea Stoeckel—everyone calls her Andi."

"She doesn't appear to have any misgivings about dishing the dirt about Diana, does she?" I asked.

"Nope," Marty responded. "Maybe we ought to drop by with one of your cakes, sweeten her up, and get the scoop."

"I've been considering something similar. This sounds like a job for mystery shoppers," I said, explaining what I meant by that and my idea about also trying to track down the scent I'd caught on the breeze near Fitzgerald's Bluff.

"Hold on!" Marty exclaimed. "I was only kidding about playing detective. If the killer saw us on the bluff that morning, all we need is to turn up at the resort asking questions about Diana. Won't that invite trouble?"

"Leave that to me," Neely replied. "I'm a master at the art of disguise. Since you don't need a posse to rescue you from the hoosegow, Miriam, how about we unleash a gang of old lady detectives on this case, instead?"

"We'll set a new standard in sleuthing! The G-O-L-D standard with our Gang of Old Lady Detectives on the case. I love it!" Charly exclaimed.

"What about Devers' warning to stay out of it?"

"Come on, Marty, cops always say that to amateur sleuths and private investigators. Who cares what he says anyway? If Diana Durand's murderer knows who we are, let's even the odds by finding out whodunit. We don't just need mystery shoppers, though. Our GOLD squad needs to be deployed on several fronts. Let me tell you what I found out today, and then I'll explain what I mean by that."

10

Scarves, Scones, and Scripts

T HE NEXT MORNING, I woke up both anxious and excited about the prospect of our undercover work. I walked Domino and then breezed through my other chores. Marty's suggestion that we go to the resort bearing gifts made sense to me, so I baked vanilla bean scones. Lots of them!

I'd keep the little boxes of scones tied up with bows as secret weapons. A little sugar might create a buzz if there was a lull in the conversation. Passing ourselves off as women in search of customers for baked goods might also help us get out of a jam if Neely and I got into one.

Baking always settles me down and helps me focus. That worked today, even though once I'd finished packing up the goodies, my mind wandered back to last night's revelations. Some, as Charly had warned, weren't very appetizing.

"She was definitely strangled—but not by hand, since there aren't any fingerprints or bruises like those you'd find on someone killed that way. Nothing abrasive like a chain or rope; something soft like a scarf, maybe."

"Okay, so that means the police don't have the scarf or

whatever else was used to kill her, right?"

"Right. There was no scarf found behind Fitzgerald's Bluff or on her body when it washed ashore at Blue Haven. So, her cell phone and the murder weapon are both missing."

"Maybe a woman owned the scarf she used to kill Diana and took it, so it couldn't be traced back to her," Marty suggested.

"It could be, but even if the scarf belonged to Diana, the killer might have taken it to prevent the police from getting any evidence left behind. Or, it could have come off while she was in the water."

"There was no scarf on her body when Domino and I found her," I said.

"That's the way I remember it, too. No scarf. That's why I could see the bruising on her neck," Midge confirmed.

"Okay. It was gone before her body went into the water, then. Who knows what other trace evidence was washed away? Diana wasn't in the water long, as we already know, but the Pacific Ocean is so chilly that it makes body temperature a less reliable way to judge how long she was dead before the killer dragged her into the ocean."

"A clever strategy for making it harder to finger the perpetrator," Midge commented.

"Yes, although it must have been early morning since she'd eaten breakfast not too long before she was killed and most of it was still in her stomach."

"Oh, yuck," Marty said.

"Let me see if I understand. Diana had breakfast at the

crack of dawn—not long before Miriam and Domino found her. Does that mean she was alone or with someone she knew?" Neely asked.

"I'm guessing she was out with someone after a night of drinking. There was alcohol in her bloodstream—not so much that she was drunk, but she'd had more than a couple of drinks."

"It makes sense that she and a drinking buddy stopped nearby after their night out on the town. There's a Denny's that's open twenty-four/seven—just off the highway. I ate there when Domino and I were on our way into town."

"The truck stop feeds people all night, too," Midge offered. "I like to have an early breakfast there occasionally and shoot the breeze with some of the truckers passing through. Doward Wilson, the head cook, serves a mean steak omelet. I'll ask him if Diana had breakfast there."

"She'd stand out in that place in her designer duds, wouldn't she?" Marty asked.

"Maybe at Denny's too. Especially now that her picture has been plastered all over in the media. Why don't I ask around about her there, too?"

"That would be great, Midge. In fact, that's what I had in mind when I said we needed to act on several fronts. Here's another issue to consider. I think the clothes she had on were more beach or resort wear rather than bar-hopping clothes, don't you? She must have had plans to spend the day at the beach with someone."

"That would explain the location of the crime scene," I said. "Maybe her evening of bar-hopping was followed by breakfast with someone who lives here at Seaview Cottages or near the beach, and they went for a stroll after they ate."

"If she and her bar-hopping pal spent the night together, maybe it's one of the other men Edgar claims she was seeing. If he lives nearby, she could have changed her clothes at his place before going to breakfast. I'm sure glad Edgar's nephew gave him an alibi."

"I hear you, Marty. Edgar's innocence doesn't mean there's not a killer in our community," Neely suggested. "The summer people have arrived and several of the cottages on the beach are rented now, too. Maybe Diana found herself a new man among the visitors and he turned out to be a psycho."

"Lots of the summer renters spend time at the Blue Haven Resort, so it's entirely possible Diana met someone there who's renting around here for the summer," Midge added.

"We could check with the people staying in the summer cottages located within walking distance of Fitzgerald's Bluff. If this wasn't her first beach date, maybe someone's seen her around there before." Charly shrugged after she made that suggestion.

"Preferably with a male companion."

"That's presuming her killer was a man, Marty. As you already pointed out, a woman could have been wearing the scarf used to kill her." Marty nodded in response to Charly's point.

"Okay, we make the rounds and ask if anyone remembers seeing her with anyone—male or female," Midge concluded.

"Sure, as long as no one goes anywhere alone," Charly

had said at that point. She'd issued the warning in such a serious manner that I got butterflies in my stomach, even now, recalling her tone. Another creepy moment from last night sent a little chill through me, too. Marty, the most anxious member of our little group had asked a question directed to no one in particular.

"What about the phone call made by Diana Durand's ghost?"

"It's not her ghost. Someone has her missing cell phone," Neely had replied immediately.

"If her killer took it, why call Edgar?" I'd wondered aloud.

"That doesn't make any sense to me, either. Maybe Joe had it right and the killer planned to get rid of the body and pretend she'd taken off for Mexico or somewhere else. If that was the intention, why not leave a voicemail or send a text message? I checked with my contact at the police station, and they've got a warrant for her phone records and permission to use the GPS device embedded in the phone to track it down. Maybe the phone or the records will clear up the matter of that ghostly call."

At that point, we'd spent the next few minutes deciding who was going to do what today. Marty planned to go with Midge to check for sightings of Diana Durand at the Denny's, the truck stop, and a local café in Duneville Downs that opens early because it only serves breakfast and then closes at two.

Neely and I were going to visit the resort this morning. After lunch, the four of us planned to meet up and then split the list Charly promised to get for us identifying the addresses for summer rental properties. Charly bowed out of the legwork to do more digging into Diana Durand and Dave Winick's backgrounds and another round of follow up with her police contacts. She was also going to track down the blogger who'd published the claim that there was a deal afoot for Blue Haven to take over our community.

"Domino, how crazy are we to be getting more involved in this trouble? Charly says Hank's competent, even if Deputy Devers isn't. Should we just stay out of it?" Domino's response was to take off for the front door. Seconds later, the doorbell rang.

"Wow! What smells so great?" Neely asked as she swept into the cottage and I closed the door behind her.

"I've been baking scones to take with us in case we get into a situation where a small bribe might help."

I stared at Neely, who had transformed herself into a resort guest. She wore an outfit that wasn't too different from the one Diana had been wearing at the time of her death. White Capri pants, a knit top, and canvas sneakers. She'd also tamed her curly hair with gel or had contained it some other way. Her wild mane was tucked up beneath a visor in a shade of blue that matched the stripe in her boatneck shirt. With the hat and a pair of enormous dark glasses she looked nothing like she had last night in her vibrant purple tunic and a pair of lounge pants like something that might be worn in a harem.

"Good thinking!" I blinked for a second trying to put Neely's comment back into context given how distracted I'd become by her new "look."

"Oh, yeah—the scones. It was Marty's idea, remember?" Neely nodded. "You want to do a taste test?"

"I thought you'd never ask!" I realized that I still hadn't moved even thought I'd made that offer of a scone. It also dawned on me that Neely carried what resembled two small overnight bags—one in each hand.

"I'm sorry I'm so out of it. You really look different and I'm trying to understand how you've done it. Can I carry one of those bags for you?"

"I'm okay. Let's eat and then we'll work on changing your look. I know there's no way the killer spotted me out on the bluff since I wasn't there. Just to be on the safe side, I figured I'd give myself a makeover too. If the strangler's been roaming around here checking up on you, I didn't want to take a chance that we were spotted together at the clubhouse or waiting to be seated in the dining room. We got lots of attention standing around with Dudley Doofus and Handsome Hank."

"You look great, Miriam!" Neely exclaimed later. "This wig makes you look ten years younger. Not that you're old at fifty. You should get contacts and dye your hair the same shade as the wig you're wearing." I was speechless when she came up with that number so glibly. What could I say?

"I'm comfortable looking my age. What makes you think I'm not fifty-five?"

"Your birthdate is on file so the HOA can send you a birthday card. It's on that form your husband filled out when he bought the Hemingway Cottage." Neely squinted a little behind her fishbowl specs that she'd put back on to do my makeover. Her brow furrowed as if puzzled by my concern. "Oh, please, our conversation about the brouha-ha among HOA board members hasn't worried you, has it? You don't have to worry about being younger than fifty-five. Unless your husband decides to divorce you or turns up dead." I gulped. Still puzzled, Neely peered at me and then shrugged.

"Come on, let's do your makeup—Hollywood diva style. Then we'll have to find something for you to wear. Do you have a tight pair of jeans?"

"Not one I bought on purpose. After the cake, Shoo Fly pie, and scones, I bet I do now." Neely laughed.

"It'll be good for you to get out of those baggy sweats you wear around here most of the time. Don't get me wrong—I like comfortable clothes more than anyone I know, but a little flair goes a long way, my child." It was my turn to have a puzzled expression on my face.

"I'm getting into character. We're going to be a mother and daughter visiting from LA. I'm Carmel Schneider, and you're Tara Brown, okay?" I giggled at the excited expression on Neely's face and wondered how on earth she'd picked those names!

"Carmel and Tara sure sound like names that could come straight out of Hollywood."

"Good! If I can work it into the conversation, I'm going to let it drop that you're on vacation writing a script and always on the lookout for the next great one someone else has written. That ought to create a bit of a buzz. When you've been on the West Coast longer, you'll understand how many Californians have a script in a drawer or are working on one—in their heads at least."

"Are you sure we want to create buzz?" I asked. Neely nodded enthusiastically.

"Buzz is always helpful when you want to get people

to talk to you. The idea that you're writing a script also gives us cover when we ask about Diana Durand's trouble. Depending on whodunit, Diana's story has made-for-TV movie written all over it. In fact, faux daughter, here's a little advice from your pseudo-mother. That might be an interesting first writing project for you—*A Body on Fitzgerald's Bluff*." My head was spinning at the pace Neely's imagination set.

"A scriptwriter from Hollywood bearing scones. Let them figure that one out!" I laughed.

"Oh, you are a West Coast newbie. California is a nation of foodies! Alongside that script stashed in a desk drawer is an old family recipe for the world's greatest something—scone, burger, cupcake, salad dressing—you name it! If you don't sell that script you've got to have something else up your sleeve." I laughed heartily. Domino, who had been lounging nearby made this little woo-woo sound as if laughing along with us.

"Let's go find your tightest pair of jeans and a breezy blouse to wear with them. You can put those reading glasses away since I have a pair of Linda Farrow cat-eye shades for you that were in a swag bag a friend sent me. Soooo trendy! You really are going to look the part."

"Linda Farrow? Cat-eye shades? Swag bag? I don't speak Californian yet, do I?" I shook my head, realizing how out to sea I still am in my new hometown.

"Pricey designer. Pointy edged shades. A bag of gifts handed out at events trendy enough to give out thousand-dollar pairs of sunglasses. That's a quick and dirty translation that will have to do for now. We've got some shopping to do. Fortunately, I also have money left on a gift card I got in exchange for a promise to review the goods at Two. That's a boutique that's chez chic. It'll help us fit the part to carry shopping bags with their logo on them as props. They sell caftans which is where I got the one I wore to Charly's. In a shop like that where most everything is size zero, it's about the only thing that fits me."

"It's beautiful and looks so comfy," I said.

"It is comfy, and it ought to be beautiful, too, for four hundred bucks. No way am I going to wear it to the beach, even though it's meant to be a cover up, you know?" I was shaking my head as that "fish out of water" feeling rushed over me again.

"Four hundred dollars for something to wear around sand and saltwater. That's impossible to believe! I'm sure I'm going to blow it in my pose as a with-it SoCal shopper when I gasp at the price tags."

"Nah—it's fine to express shock and outrage at prices. Whining is okay, too! On the way to Blue Haven, I'll coach you on how to whine as if you were born and raised in the San Fernando Valley. Let's glam you up with my movie star makeup tricks. You're going to be a Hollywood hottie by the time I'm done with you!"

11

A Bad Boy Shopper?

OUR FIRST COUPLE of stops on our mystery shopper adventure turned out to be duds. I'd spotted the Caswell-Massey cologne shop that the website had listed among all the stores at the resort. It carries men and women's fragrances. Pete had a cologne he used, off and on, for years after we visited their store in Cleveland. I was inspired as I explained this to Neely on our way.

"Maybe I noticed the fragrance out there on the beach because I smelled it before in that Cleveland store."

"It's worth a try. Let's check," Neely said.

After fifteen minutes, I gave up. Nothing came close. Neely suggested it might not have been a man's cologne. After a similar effort sampling a few women's perfumes, I could barely distinguish one fragrance from another.

"That's because you have 'nose fatigue.' That's why some people wear too much perfume. When your nose gets too full of a fragrance, you need to give it a rest. All the little receptors are tuckered out. Even if you switch from one fragrance to another, the colognes are likely to share some of the same base elements."

"Time for a break, huh?" I asked. Neely nodded and

led us out of the shop.

I tried not to let my discouragement show. A few minutes later, when we passed a Brooks Brother's clothing store that carried several proprietary fragrances, I tried again. We had no luck there either.

"Oh well, what difference will it make if we discover which fragrance it is? It's not likely to put us any closer to knowing *who* wore it." I sighed heavily. "I hope this mystery shopper idea won't be a complete waste of your time."

"Chin up, Tara, my daughter. We're just getting started! The gift card I have is burning a hole in my pocket. We'll look much more the part if we're carrying bags from a posh place like Two." Neely darted off and then pushed her way into the small store. The pencil-thin waif slouching on a bar stool near the register took one look at us and went back to scrolling through pictures or messages on her cell phone.

"Holler if I can help you," she said with her eyes downcast. She must have assumed we were merely browsing or killing time. At least she wasn't giving us the hard sell that I'd experienced in some of the mall stores in Ohio.

"Will do! You must be reading about that dead woman they found on the beach. She worked here, didn't she?"

"Not in this shop," she replied without even looking up.

"I heard she was a shopaholic. She must have shopped in a cutting-edge place like this, right? In LA, everyone is talking about Two. That's how I got this great gift card in my A-List Swag Bag at the premiere of *Mindy's Mark*."

Neely glanced at me as she embellished her story about how she got her hands on that gift card. Given my track record when it comes to fibbing, I wasn't going to correct her.

The young woman's demeanor changed at the mention of gift card. Or it could have been Neely's reference to the swag bag or the mega-hit movie. The sales clerk put her phone down and took a closer look at us.

"Are you looking for something specific or just browsing?" She asked sweetly as she handed each of us a business card.

"I have a gorgeous caftan I bought at Two in LA already. I'm going to buy another one in a different color. Maybe you could help my daughter, Tara, find something cool and trendy." Then *"Mom"* leaned in and lowered her voice before glibly continuing the fabricated story she was telling. "Tara's working on a movie script about that young woman's murder. It would really help her with character development if you could give her some idea of the sort of thing Diana Durand would have worn."

"I can definitely do that. Follow me." I glanced at Neely with raised eyebrows in mock surprise at the series of lies she'd just spit out without hesitation and uttered as though she'd scripted the entire situation. The transformation in her personality was far more stunning to me than the changes she'd made to her appearance. She smiled and made hand motions urging me to hurry after the woman who, according to her business card, was Valerie Bargewell. I did a quick attitude adjustment and got into my role.

"You're a lifesaver, Valerie. I can't tell you how much I

need to get a handle on the woman's style and motivation to portray her as a well-rounded character. People will want to understand who she was, although so far the media hasn't portrayed her as a very sympathetic character."

"Sympathetic character's not how I'd describe her, either. Murdered on a beach isn't a good end for anyone, is it?" She shrugged and moved on.

"No, it's not," I replied. A brightly colored scarf in a gauzy fabric caught my eye. "This is fun, isn't it?"

"Yeah, she bought several of those." There wasn't much enthusiasm in Valerie's tone. Maybe the scarf was too cheap for the salesclerk to get excited about. I glanced at the price tag and felt woozy. Three hundred dollars and Diana had purchased several of them.

"Is 'fun' no better than 'sympathetic' as a way to characterize Diana Durand?"

"Not unless you're referring to the fun of the hunt."

"The hunt?" I asked and paused for a second. "As in men, you mean?"

"Yes. Here's an outfit she bought." In a flash, Valerie had pulled an ankle-length wisp of a dress with spaghetti straps from the rack in a black nearly sheer fabric. She paired it with silver sandals and a foldable white hat with black trim." I watched with amazement as she pulled more outfits together—skinny pants with tops that somehow managed to be slinky even though they were made of the same tissue-paper-like fabric. A little on the scanty side for my taste.

"Judging by the ensembles you're putting together her coworker wasn't making it up when she called Diana a siren, was she?" Valerie pursed her lips and shrugged.

"She definitely dressed to attract attention."

"It sure looks like the wardrobe you'd own if you intended to lead men to their destruction," Neely commented, suddenly appearing at my elbow.

"I wouldn't know what Diana Durand did with the men once she had them in her sights," Valerie said. "Truthfully, I don't much care what our customers do with the clothes I sell them. The reason I mentioned Diana Durand was on 'the hunt' is that the first time we met, she asked me if I'd seen any good-looking men around the resort lately. Since she was with a man at the time, her question stuck in my mind as predatory. I'm not sure about the siren thing. If all the men she bagged were like the big guy who came in here with her, I'm guessing they could take care of themselves."

"What makes you say that?" I asked as nonchalantly as I could. My heart had sped up as she spoke.

"The guy was huge. Not just tall, but well-built, in his thirties, maybe, but his face had a story to tell that I didn't want to hear. Bad boy was written all over him with scars and tattoos—even on his head that he'd shaved. He was tame enough sitting in the corner hanging onto the bags she had with her from other shops."

"Did he pick up the tab?" I asked.

"No, she put everything on account. Several thousand dollars as I recall." Valerie shrugged. That lightheaded feeling returned as I imagined slashing the balance on my car loan in half with the money Diana spent on one purchase.

"Thanks, Valerie. This has been very enlightening."

Neely picked up that black dress with the spaghetti straps and the white hat and added it to several items she was already holding. "You'll look great in that dress."

"How do you know it'll even fit?" I gasped.

"Don't worry. It's one size fits all," Valerie replied. She glanced at Neely. "Fits most."

"Get her a hat and a pair of those sandals, too, okay?" Neely made eye contact and then paused. She had to be waiting for me to jump in with my shoe size. I did that quickly before our salesperson had time to wonder why mom didn't rattle off her daughter's shoe size.

"Ring us up, okay?" Neely asked, obviously ready to leave.

When we left the store, I was still reeling from the tale of the tape. Neely's shopping spree hadn't reached the several thousand-dollar mark like that set by Diana Durand, but a couple more items would have done it.

"Thanks for your generosity, Neely. You shouldn't have done that."

"Hey, it's good to have friends in Hollywood. I can only fit into the larger version of one size fits all garments as that salesclerk so deftly pointed out. What else could I buy in there for me besides a second caftan, a beach bag, and a floppy hat? You'll be *tres chic* in that dress. You'll also look so much better in the red caftan than I would. The gold one's for me! Purple and gold are my colors as I'm sure you've noticed." Neely handed me a shopping bag with the Two logo on it.

"Here! Help your dear old mother, please, and carry your own bag. Let's pay a visit to the shop where Diana worked next. Maybe we'll learn more there."

"How much money was Edgar spending on Diana?" I asked trying to keep up with Neely as she sped off toward our next shopping destination. "Valerie said she already had shopping bags with her!"

"Too much, that's for sure. You're wondering about an account that allowed her to purchase several thousand dollars' worth of designer goodies in one fell swoop, aren't you?"

"Yes, I am. Not to mention the fact she's got a man with her while she's spending Edgar's money. How could she do that to a sweet old guy like him?"

"A sugar daddy, too sweet for his own good. In a way, it serves him right for getting mixed up with her. At least Edgar came to his senses."

"Thank goodness!" I exclaimed. "Given the company she keeps, Edgar may be lucky to be alive."

"I'm inclined to agree with you given Valerie Bargewell's description of Diana's shopping companion. He must be the same guy Alf and Alyssa witnessed Diana slapping in the parking lot. I know they said it was about money, but it could have been a lover's quarrel as well."

"Tagging along with Diana on one of her shopping sprees sounds like boyfriend behavior. On the other hand, a bad boy shopper doesn't quite fit the image of a man with scars and tattoos, does it?"

"It might if Diana met him in the music business. It's possible he's mixed up in the whole West Coast hip-hop, gangster rap music scene."

"The what? I asked.

"Oh, please. They have rap music in Ohio. Eminem spent lots of his formative years in the Midwest." Then she made a few sounds that were more buzzes and bumps than musical notes. I nodded, even though I only vaguely understood what she was trying to tell me.

"I've heard of rap and Eminem, but Adele and Annie Lennox are more my speed. If you say he could be a musician, I trust you."

"A bodyguard or a roadie rather than a performer is more likely," Neely retorted and then pondered the matter a little more. "He could be a poser or a hanger-on—you know? Someone trying to look the part and insinuate himself into a performer's entourage. I'm sure the Bay Area has their share of those just like LA."

"What would that get him—especially after her music career ended?" I asked.

"It's hard to say, although a cut of what Edgar was coughing up wasn't chump change." With that, Neely opened the door and ushered me into the Blue Moon Boutique.

This shop was much larger than Two had been. A wider range of resort wear was on display, including items for men and women, as well as a section for children. The décor was lovely, skillfully blending shades of blue with other beach colors. A soothing blend of ambient music and pounding waves invited shoppers to linger. What a tour de force of the California laid back motif!

Laid back didn't apply to the saleswomen on duty in the nearly empty shop. The moment we walked in, both clerks eyed us. When they spotted the bags we carried, they headed toward us. Like two outfielders aiming to catch the same flyball, they were on what appeared to be a collision course.

"I've got this," the older of the two women said—like an outfielder calling for the ball. The younger woman got the message and backed off.

"May I help you?" The nametag pinned to her shirt told us her name was Penney.

"I hope you can. My daughter, Tara, is looking for something to lounge around in while she's on a pretend vacation. All she's done so far is work—reading one script after another, trying to get inspired to write her own." I took my cue from Neely's mention of script-writing.

"A working vacation is still a vacation, Mom."

"We bought a gorgeous caftan for her at Two, but I want to buy her yoga pants or something that might remind her that she's supposed to be working out, too, not just holed up in our suite writing about murder."

"Murder?" Penney asked.

"Yes. Tara's putting a script together for a TV movie about the death of that young woman—Lady Di—that's what I used to call her, anyway. She was gorgeous and so kind when I was in here before. Diana had the best taste, too. I can't believe she's been murdered. Why would anyone do such a thing?" Penney raised her eyebrows as if skeptical or surprised by what Neely was saying about Diana.

"The police asked me that question and I told them I don't know. Diana Durand wasn't the easiest person to get along with, but if every spoiled brat at the resort got killed, the beaches around here would be littered with bodies."

I must have done the very thing I feared I would do when we'd cooked up this charade—reacted in an un-laid-back way to the saleswoman's uncharitable remark. Penney picked up on it and frowned. Then she turned us over to her coworker, perhaps concluding that we were more interested in gossip than shopping. Even though that happened to be the truth, the sudden dismissiveness in her manner bothered me. In any case, Penney was done with us.

"Andi knew her better than I did. If you want the scoop on Lady Di, she'll give it to you." My heart thumped a little harder realizing we may have just run into one of the women we hoped might indeed have plenty to share with us about Diana Durand. Andi had closed in on us as soon as she heard the word murder. Now she stepped forward and spoke to us.

"I'd be happy to chat with you if you don't mind waiting for me until I get back from my break. I need a cup of coffee."

"That's great, Andi. I'm Carmel Schneider, by the way," Neely said going back into undercover liar mode. "Why don't we go with you? We could use a break too. I'm getting too old for this shop 'til you drop' routine."

"It has nothing to do with age, Mom. I'm ready for caffeine. These scones are calling to me too." I pulled out one of the little boxes I had stashed in a large, colorful canvas tote Neely had loaned me. All my tote bags have grocery store names and logos on them and Neely hadn't considered them Blue Haven Resort worthy.

"Do you enjoy scones, Penney?" I asked. "I baked these myself—vanilla bean." The saleslady smirked in a "yeah right" kind of way.

"In your hotel suite?" She asked in a sarcastic tone.

Quick on her feet, Neely had a snappy reply. She giggled in a high-pitched voice and slapped her side. At that moment, Neely was spectacular in her performance as the daffy old dame from LA. I could see how the deputy could fall for it as Midge had said.

"You are too funny! She baked those yesterday before we drove up here for our getaway. Here, try one!" Neely grabbed the box from my hand, ripped the ribbon off, opened the top, and offered its contents to the salesclerk. The rich, sweet aroma that escaped from the box was like a magic elixir. A faint smile that had appeared on Penney's face turned to bliss once she took a bite of the glaze-covered scone.

"Mm," she murmured. Andi shook her head and motioned for us to follow her.

"I'll bring you back something to drink—coffee or tea?"

"Milk, please," Penney replied in a voice muffled by a mouthful of that scone and the mellow mood that had settled over her.

"Sure," Andi replied as we stepped out of the shop and the door shut behind us. "Heck, if I'd known the taming of the shrew could be that easy, I'd have learned to bake long ago. I mean, how hard can it be?"

Neely sent me a sideways glance with one eyebrow arched as if she was about to lose her laid-back mojo. I shook my head slightly, and then took the lead hoping to keep us on an amiable track.

"She does seem to be a little cranky," I said.

That's when a familiar fragrance hit me. My heart pounded as my body went on alert. I searched around me wondering where it had come from. Several people milled about, but no one appeared to be paying attention to us. I took a couple of deep breaths of air. The scent had gone as quickly as it had come. Neely noticed, but Andi didn't.

"Ha!" Andi said. "That's an understatement."

"I bet it's not easy working with her, is it?" Neely, back in her motherly mode, asked.

"No, it is not! Penney Wilfort has an ax to grind. My guess is that she didn't always have to work for a living—not as a salesclerk anyway. It's not as easy as it looks to act as if the 'customer's always right,' you know?" Neely nodded sympathetically.

Andi stopped and opened a door that led outside of the enclosed mall area to a boardwalk. On our right was a small kiosk selling coffee, espresso, and other beverages. We placed our orders and grabbed seats around a small bistro table as Andi asked us to do while she waited for the beverages.

"What was that about?" Neely asked me when we were seated.

"I caught a whiff of that scent."

"The one the strangler wore?" I nodded.

"That's not good," Neely replied doing a quick scan of the area around us.

"I didn't see anyone stalking us. Did you?" I asked.

12

A Man Named Boo

NEELY SHOOK HER head no in response to my question about a stalker. Andi slid into a chair opposite me ending the discussion. The coffee and scones soon had Andi spilling the beans at breakneck speed. That's after I agreed to call her later with the scone recipe. I don't find scones the easiest treats to bake, but far be it from me to disabuse the young woman of her view that baking is always "a piece of cake."

"Diana went through men as if they were library books she borrowed and then returned. A little dogeared and worse for wear, too. I figured it was only a matter of time before one of the men decided to resist being dumped in a book return. She didn't always return one book before checking out another one, if you get my drift."

"I believe I do. Lady Di was no lady, was she?" I asked. "She sure had you snookered, Mom." Neely shrugged.

"It wouldn't be the first time. I never saw her with a man or I might have formed a different opinion of her. She must have put on quite a show around here for you to know so much about her problems with men."

"Are you kidding? It was like a soap opera. Men coming and going—sometimes only minutes apart. You'll love this! She even bought them the same gifts. Can you imagine two of them showing up at the same time in identical aloha shirts?" Then Andi glanced around to make sure we were alone. "I didn't tell this to the reporter, but Diana had a fling with an exec here at Blue Haven. Technically, he wasn't her supervisor, so I'm not sure they broke any rules. They must not have been worried since they didn't hide it. I saw him pick her up in the parking lot when her shift was over—more than once. Diana went on and on about Dave this and Dave that for weeks. Then it ended. Given her interest in monied men, he should have been a keeper."

"What happened?" I asked.

"She found a better prospect in this poor old guy at Seaview. He called her 'Dee' and she called him 'E' most of the time. I figured his days were numbered once she sank her claws into him. I was floored when she showed us a picture with her 'sweet little ol' sugar daddy,' as she called Edgar Humphrey with his white hair and all duded up like Mark Twain."

"I take it that means she wasn't shy about telling you his name. Wasn't she worried you or someone else might cut in on her? Or afraid that he might resent being called her sugar daddy if word got back to him?" Andi let out a little puff of air and looked at Neely as if she were crazy.

"Lady Di? Worried about competition for a man or his feelings? Please! Now that you mention it, though, she didn't actually give me his name." Andi sipped her coffee and finished the scone she'd been eating. She was obviously ticked. I feared we were going to lose her before we heard anything much that wasn't "old news" since Dave and Edgar were names we already had.

"Have another, won't you? Your break can't be over yet." I pushed that open box toward her. "I really would like to hear more of what you have to say since most of the information I've gotten so far is thin. Sanitized, too, apparently. They didn't name you in that news story, but my guess is you're the one who gave them the scoop that Diana was a siren, leading men to their ruin on the rocks."

"Yep! That was me—not that I want my name to get around. I kept Diana's secrets while she was alive. I'm going to lay it all on the line when the police interview me tomorrow. What else do you want to know? Off the record, of course."

"Well, how did you get Edgar Humphrey's real name?"

"He had 'surprises' sent to her at the store and I saw his name on the deliveries. Diana told us he set up an account for her here at the resort, so in addition to all the gifts, she could shop on her lunch breaks. I'm not sure how she blew it, but he's the one guy who used that book return on her! Was she ever furious. He has no idea how lucky he is to be alive."

"What goes around comes around," Neely muttered. "When you said she had more than one library book out at a time, are you saying she was two-timing Edgar or someone else?"

"Edgar, for sure. That's my best guess about how she lost her sugar daddy."

"Was she still seeing the resort exec?" I asked.

"Possibly. He came in here to get her out of trouble more than once, even after she'd moved on."

"It must mean there were no hard feelings once they split up if he was willing to help her, right?" Neely asked.

"I guess so," Andi replied.

"What kind of trouble was she in?" I asked even though I already had some idea about what it might be.

"Penney Wilfort was Diana's immediate supervisor. She reported Diana to the shop manager for being a screw up on the job."

"As in turning up late or calling off work?" Neely asked.

"Yes. She was always late getting to work or coming back from breaks, leaving early, or ditching work—you name it. When the shop manager wrote Diana up and gave her a formal reprimand, Dave Winick stepped in. That's one reason Penney's so cranky about young women she regards as 'brats.' Penney was told in no uncertain terms that she should lay off Diana."

"Wow! That would make me more than a little cranky. Paranoid, too." I commented.

"Penney did as she was told until stuff started to disappear from the store. She suspected Diana was up to no good, although she wasn't going to go out on a limb again after Winick warned her."

"No way!" Neely exclaimed.

"Oh, yes, and it gets worse. Penney called us all together for a meeting and advised us that she was going to have security do spot checks of the drawers where we keep our personal items stashed during the day. You'd think that would have scared Diana to death, but goods kept disappearing. A couple of weeks ago, when Penney had security do one of those checks, they found merchandise in the drawer used by another employee. She was fired on the spot even though she claimed she didn't know anything about the items or how they got in there. I swear I saw Diana smirk."

"Do you know the name of the person who got fired? Revenge could be a motive for murder."

"Yes. I don't suppose there's any way to spare her more trouble, is there? Promise me you won't smear her name—if anything, it would be nice to clear it, wouldn't it?"

A different side of Andi Stoeckel had suddenly appeared. I let go of my initial concern that she was a jealous coworker trying to besmirch Diana's name out of spite. She appeared to be deeply distressed by the injustice her friend had suffered.

"I'd love for the truth to come out. Diana was a troubled woman; it would be great if her death brought about a little good for someone she wronged along the way." Andi nodded in agreement with me and then sighed sadly.

"Her name is Judi Stephenson. I have a phone number for her. I'll call her first and tell her it's okay to talk to you. I'm not sure what she can add, but she can at least make sure I got the facts right about her story."

"I'd love to speak to her if she's willing. I think you mentioned in that news story that Diana had a singing career in the Bay area. Did she talk about that?"

"Oh yes. Endlessly at first. She ended up here on the Central Coast because she was the victim of a horrible betrayal that put a halt to her singing career. Poor innocent Diana found out another singer had set her up by telling her agent's wife that they were having a fling. The wife was livid, threatened to ruin her if she didn't leave town. Blah, blah, blah."

"No threats to kill her, though?" Neely asked.

"Whoa! That's a good question. None that she shared with me. I never bothered to check to see how much of a career there was to ruin. She claimed she had lots of gigs at local clubs in the Bay area, but with Diana, you just never knew what was true. I figured she'd finally run out of steam about her San Francisco troubles until some guy showed up a few weeks ago and it started up again."

"Her agent?" Neely asked.

"No. This was a big, ugly guy with a face that had seen more than a few bar fights. My first thought was that she'd borrowed what they call 'hard money'—like from a loan shark, you know?"

"Yeah, I understand what you mean." My stomach did a little flip-flop as I spoke. Unfortunately, I do know what hard money is. The back-alley negotiations portrayed in movies are overly melodramatic since hard money's a term for private loans, often made at higher interest rates than bank loans, and backed by assets like our house. Hard money's not always legit.

If Alf and Alyssa got it wrong, maybe he was demanding money from Diana when they witnessed that altercation in the parking lot. Slapping him wasn't the best way to win an argument with a bill collector like him. Still, if he'd been provoked enough to strangle her, he wouldn't have needed to use a scarf.

"So, who was he?" Neely asked.

"A business partner from San Francisco, according to Diana. I wish I could tell you what kind of business that involved. And, before you can ask, the only name I got was 'Boo,' believe it or not."

"Are you sure?" Neely gasped.

"Yes. 'Boo as in big and scary, but he's a marshmallow,' was Diana's explanation. Odd, huh?"

"Now you're the one understating things," I said.

"Oh shoot!" Andi said, looking at her watch. "I'd better get back with that milk Penney wanted before she decides to write me up."

"Okay, can I call you later if I have questions?"

"Sure." Andi gave me her number and I typed it into my cell phone. I pulled out another box of scones and slid it across the table.

"To tame the shrew until you start baking your own."

"Thanks, Tara. Don't forget to call me with the recipe, okay? We've only covered the tip of the iceberg when it comes to men. I'll think about it and I'll write the names down." Her use of my fake name jarred me for an instant. I'd have to be sure to remember to use it when I called her.

"I'm sure the police will be interested in every name you can give them," I said. "I will, too."

"I can give you three more names off the top of my head—Mark Hudson, Howard Humphrey, and Mike Evans."

"Humphrey? That's the same last name as her sugar daddy," Neely observed.

"It is—his nephew. I told you Diana was a two-timer. As I recall, she was friendly with Howard before he introduced her to Edgar. Howard's one of the books she dumped in the book return as far as I can tell, but he still came in here a few times after Uncle Edgar became her sugar daddy. 'He's going to be family,' she told me once." Andi laughed. "I was even more surprised when Howard showed up again after she broke up with Edgar. What a piece of work she was, huh?"

All I could do was nod in affirmation. My imagination failed me when I tried to understand what on earth a woman like Diana was doing. The list of people angry enough to kill her was a long one. It could grow even longer depending on how much truth there was to Andi's "tip of the iceberg" comment about men.

After another report of the big man turning up in Diana's life, Boo held the top spot on that growing list. He and Diana were up to something—but what? I had the same question about Howard Humphrey, who was next in line on the list of suspects that now also included a woman's name—Judi Stephenson. Why not seek revenge against the woman who set her up?

13

Blue Shue Bribery

"**H**OWARD HUMPHREY. HOW do you like that?" Neely asked.

"I don't like it one bit. That's all Edgar needs is to hear that his nephew is as untrustworthy as his ex-girlfriend was before someone ended her wretched life. Edgar cared for her more than he's willing to admit, don't you think?"

"Yeah, he's a big dope to fall for young women the way he does. Fortunately, he's a fool who sets limits. Since Edgar used Howard as an alibi, that gives Howard one, too."

"You're right. Edgar's nephew may be a louse, but that doesn't make him a strangler," I conceded.

"We'll have Charly check him out. If Howard stands to inherit part or all of Edgar's estate, he could have been involved with Diana in some unscrupulous way."

"Like speeding Edgar along to an early grave in order to get his hands on his inheritance quicker?" I asked.

"It wouldn't be the first time that sort of ambition was a motive for murder. History is full of examples of murderous conflicts over rights to the throne back when an heir stood to inherit an entire kingdom. Something was going on, and I'm not sure Edgar should continue to rely on Howard as a trusted companion even though he is family as Diana pointed out." Neely's shoulders slumped. The idea made me sad too.

"Poor Edgar. Money's a curse, isn't it?"

"Ah, yes, that's true whether you have too much or too little," Neely responded.

"It's too bad we don't have a better name than Boo for the big ugly guy spotted with Diana. If anybody needs to be investigated it's him, isn't it?" I asked.

"Well, if the police find him as interesting as we do, they can have *The* Gardeners and Andi Stoeckel help them come up with a sketch. Or maybe there are surveillance tapes at the resort that the authorities can get their hands on. A guy like him may already be known to the police in San Francisco. With a photo or sketch, they might be able to pull up his real name."

"Now that you have me in character as a Hollywood scriptwriter, it occurs to me that Boo sounds awfully theatrical. Maybe it's a stage name."

"For what? The WWE?"

"What's the WWE?" I asked.

"The World Wrestling Entertainment."

"Are you talking about those staged fights between huge men in outlandish makeup and costumes?"

"That's not far-fetched, is it?" Neely replied. "It could be where he got the scars. Even when fight scenes are choreographed, accidents happen. I've seen stunt men get injured when there's a misstep on a well-planned stunt." Neely grew quiet for a second. "You know, Tara my Hollywood daughter, Andi made a good point when she described Boo to us. He's more likely to be a bouncer. Diana must have run into guys like him at the clubs where she sang. That could also be where Boo had the fights that left his face messed up."

"What kind of business would she have had with him—if what she told Andi was true?" Neely had a quick reply this time.

"Nothing too original. A petty scam like stealing money or credit card numbers from customers while Diana plied the poor saps with drinks and her prettiest smile. Or, you know what? Maybe Boo hocked or sold the merchandise Diana stole from the Blue Moon Boutique before Judi Stephenson was framed and fired!"

"Of course! Diana had to get rid of the stuff somehow. When I call Judi, I'll ask what they found in her drawer. That could give us some idea of how much money Diana and Boo were making from her thieving."

"While you have the poor Stephenson woman on the phone, ask her if she knows when those thefts started. I wonder if Lady Di was using the account Edgar set up to buy designer label goodies and sell them to bring in a little extra income and then switched to stealing to keep the cash rolling in."

"That would explain Boo's willingness to be her shopping companion, wouldn't it? She shops, hands the stuff over to him, and he sells it. I'm not sure how—like out of the trunk of his car?"

"Online maybe—eBay or Craig's list. They were peddling real designer goods, not knockoffs, so he could have had outlets in shops, too. I'm not sure how the black-market in designer goods works, or how much she and

Boo could have made from cashing in her loot."

"Whatever the amount, Diana could have been in a real fix when Edgar cut her off. In her desperation, pinching items from the store might have seemed reasonable."

"I doubt Diana was motivated by desperation. She spent lots of her young life engaged in underhanded activities. Some people get hooked on the cheap thrills from putting one over on others or setting them up the way she framed Judi. I don't understand it," Neely said removing her glasses and rubbing her eyes as if trying to bring the bizarre concept into better focus.

"I suppose that old proverb must be true for some people—that *stolen waters are sweet.*" I was struggling with it too given how much distress Diana must have caused Judi. "It wouldn't be a proverb, would it, if there was some truth to it?"

"It's as good an explanation as any for how Diana could get into so much trouble at such a young age. Not to mention, causing so much misery for other people. Getting fired was bad, but Judi's lucky she didn't go to jail," Neely responded.

"If Diana did frame her coworker, someone must have warned her in advance. Otherwise, how would she have known a security check was coming, so she could put the stuff in Judi Stephenson's drawer?"

"That solves another problem I've been pondering which is why Judi didn't spot the stuff in her drawer when she went on break or to lunch that day. If Diana got a heads up about the raid shortly before it happened, she could have made the transfer minutes before security arrived. Hmm..." Neely didn't ask the question we both must have had been mulling over. Who warned Diana? A moment later, we made eye contact, and then spoke almost in unison.

"A boyfriend!"

"An insider in security maybe." Neely agreed, nodding enthusiastically.

"We have a little more time before we meet Marty and Midge. Let's check out a few of the other places where Diana might have shopped. I'd like to get a better idea about how she used the resort account Edgar set up for her. I'm not sure how to bring it up or what we might learn, but maybe someone knows more about Diana's other men friends. Do you have more scones?"

"Yes."

"Good! Let's start a few doors down at Blue Shue where she must have bought the Gucci sneakers she had on when she was killed." Neely took a box of scones, and as we walked into the swanky shoe shop, she untied the ribbon. She marched right up to the saleswoman standing behind the counter and popped the top open.

"Sorry, you can't eat food in here," the young woman said. Then the sweet vanilla scent must have hit her. "Where did you buy those?"

"We didn't buy them. My daughter, Tara is a primo baker—they're homemade glazed vanilla bean scones. Want one?" She glanced around at the nearly empty store.

"Why not? I'm starving and it's not time for my lunch break yet." When she bit into the scone, she was a goner. There's no greater pleasure for a baker than to see the sugary bliss take hold of someone. I smiled. After she swallowed that bite, she spoke.

"These are wonderful! I wish we had pastries this good around here." She took another bite as I checked out the shop in which we stood. It wasn't large, but it was luxuriously appointed. The walls and shelves were emblazoned with designer labels—some I recognized, others were new to me.

"How can I help you?" She asked as she pulled a bottle of water from behind the counter. I did a quick little shuffle in my head—from scriptwriter to wannabe pastry shop owner.

"I'm considering opening a shop. I heard an employee here was murdered and her body was found on the beach. Should I be worried about that?"

"Diana Durand's troubles had nothing to do with her job, trust me."

"How do you know?" Neely asked.

"What I heard is that she left San Francisco owing lots of people money. It's no wonder since she was a shopaholic. She had an account some guy set up for her last year and she always hit empty before the end of the month when he put more money into it. Diana Durand did not treat you well if you were the one who gave her the bad news that she didn't have enough money in her account to buy whatever it was she plopped down at the register. She had a nasty mouth on her, too."

"Do you think a coworker caught her alone on the beach and decided to shut her up?" Neely peered at the twenty-something woman in a chic tunic that looked a lot like those we'd seen at Two.

"If that were the case, someone would have done it

months ago. A while back, her account permanently went to zero and Diana couldn't hassle any of us anymore."

"No kidding? Her benefactor cut her off?" Neely asked, feigning ignorance about Edgar's behavior.

"Ha! Benefactor's one name for it. I figure the guy who set up that account wised up, ended the relationship, and her shopping—on his dime, anyway." She leaned in and dropped her voice a little. "Diana soaked him for thousands while she played the field with other men in the outfits he bought for her. He had to be steamed when he found out."

"No!" I exclaimed. "You don't mean steamed enough to kill her, do you?" I asked, trying to keep the conversation going even though we already had the scoop on Edgar. Benefactor, yes. Killer, no.

"Who knows? A jealous boyfriend is the oldest story in the book when it comes to murder, isn't it?"

"Yes. Do you know who set up that account for her?" Neely asked.

"I'm not sure, but some really old rich guy was with her once or twice when she went on shopping sprees. I didn't catch his name, but I know someone who did. Diana had the nerve to introduce him to one of the guys she was sneaking around with behind his back!"

"No way!" I gasped.

"Does he work here?" Neely asked. The salesclerk nodded.

"Yes. Mark Hudson sells merchandise at the golf shop, but he also gives lessons. That's who Diana said he was when she introduced him to the old guy—her golf instructor. Mark told me he felt bad about it. She did take a couple of lessons from him before they hooked up. Mark said she paid for them with money in the account that old guy or some other chump set up for her. A woman like Diana Durand is lucky to have lived as long as she did."

"Do you think Mark Hudson would talk to us about it?" The young woman frowned a little, perhaps puzzling over my request. Neely shoved the box of scones closer.

"You keep these for later. Thanks for filling us in. Let's hope Tara feels comfortable enough about what's gone on here at Blue Haven to open a shop, so you can buy more."

"I guess you shouldn't just take my word for it. Tell Mark Hudson, Vicki Hardman says you and your mom are cool. He's a sucker for sweets, so do the same thing you did with me—bribe him." Then she beamed a beautiful sparkling white smile, exposing a Hollywood-worthy set of perfect teeth.

"Capped," Charly had said when I'd mentioned Greta Bishop's gorgeous smile. "It's a glamor thing," she'd added. A glamor thing that costs a pretty penny. I tried not to think about the fact that I'd put dental visits on hold until I could afford the insurance premiums again. I checked my bag which now held only one more box of scones.

"Thanks, Ms. Hardman," I said.

"It's Vicki, Tara. I aim to be on a first name basis if you open a shop around here. You can thank me with more of these. Do they come with chocolate chips?" I laughed.

"Yes, Vicki, they do!" As we left, I wished I could open a shop. I'm not sure how I'd explain the name change if I showed up again as Miriam rather than Tara.

Oh well, stop worrying about it, I chastised myself. It must cost a fortune to do that in an upscale resort setting like this one. There's no better way to make shoppers feel happy and comfortable than to have the enticing aroma of fresh-baked cookies or pies wafting through the air. A dreamy feeling lingered as I tagged along behind Neely. Why not? Dreaming is free.

Neely turned the corner and stopped in front of the Blue Haven Pro Shop. As soon as we entered the store, Neely made a beeline for the tall sandy-haired store clerk in a golf shirt and shorts.

"Are you Mark Hudson?" She asked.

"Who wants to know?" He replied sporting another of those big, gleaming glamor smiles.

14

All in the Family

"VICKI HARDMAN TOLD us you could answer some questions for us."

"She did, huh? What about?" His smile had faded, replaced by an expression somewhere between curiosity and suspicion.

"Yep. She told us to offer you a bribe, too." Neely went through her routine, introducing us by our fake names, and offering Mark Hudson a scone. She skipped the scriptwriter angle. Instead, she explained that I was interested in opening a bake shop, but concerned about the murder of a resort employee.

"Vicki Hardman told us you could back up her claim that Diana Durand's death wasn't related to problems here at the resort." As we stood there talking, I noticed an older man in the shop checking over a list. When he peered at us, there was something familiar about him. When he caught me looking at him, he smiled and then went back to examining his list.

"Hey, Howard, I'm going to catch an early lunch, okay?" I caught Neely's eye. She nodded.

"Yes, that's Howard," Neely whispered. He was eying

us again, peering at Neely this time. They must have run into each other before. Did he recognize her despite her makeover? I held my breath until we left the shop—waiting for Howard to out us with a "Hey, Neely, is that you?"

"I'm going to grab a sandwich and a drink to go with dessert. What do you want to know about Diana?"

"Was she a two-timer?" I asked.

"Wow! You get right to the point, don't you?" Mark asked, flashing that smile at me. "Yes. I didn't know that at first. She was beautiful, fun to be with, but heartless. At least I figured her out quick."

"When she introduced you as her golf instructor, you mean?"

"Vicki told you about that too, huh? Why do you need to talk to me if you already know I was sneaking around with her behind that nice old guy's back?" Mark Hudson appeared to be genuinely distressed as he stopped walking and looked directly at me. I felt sorry for him. A little guilty, too, about misleading him to get information since he, like Vicki Hardman, was so forthcoming.

"It sounded to us like she took you for ride. I'm not judging you. I just want to find out what happened to Diana Durand," I said.

"I wish I could tell you. I'd rest easier if I knew who killed her. Howard's Uncle Edgar had reason to do it, didn't he? If you read the news coverage, you'll find out she wasn't killed here, but near where the frail old guy lives in a retirement community a few miles north of us. That ought to ease your mind about opening a shop here at Blue Haven Resort." He shrugged.

"By the way you describe him, it doesn't sound like he could kill anyone," I said in a skeptical tone.

"No, but he could have had someone do it for him." Mark scanned the empty marble laden halls that led between the resort shops. "He might not have even had to ask. His nephew's a bigger fool than Edgar or me."

"What does that mean?" Neely prodded as Mark started walking again.

"Howard had a thing for Diana a while back. I thought it had ended or I wouldn't have started seeing her. When I found out she'd dumped Howard for his rich uncle, that shocked me more than realizing she was cheating on Edgar with me. I told Howard he'd better warn his uncle about her if he cared about him."

"Did he do that?"

"They broke up, didn't they?" Mark asked, and then paused. "Look, I don't know for certain what happened because I told Diana I didn't want to see her anymore—not as a customer or a girlfriend. Howard was really upset about it. That's awful, isn't it, wondering if a guy I work with killed someone? Since I was involved with Diana, too, I'm in no position to point fingers at anyone, am I? I'll bet everyone she dated is a suspect." Mark stopped at the door to a little café and shook his head.

"Even death doesn't end the trouble some women can cause, does it? That's probably not a very kind thing to say, but once I found out about her, I asked around. I was shocked to hear how many people she hurt."

"Edgar and Howard, you mean?" Neely asked. Mark opened the door and a blast of food odors hit us. Something spicy in a slightly exotic way. We stepped inside with him.

"Not just them, but I heard this woman, Judi Stephenson, got set up by Diana just like a guy I know in Guest Services who took guests' luggage to their room while they were checking in." Mark dropped his voice before he spoke again. "The resort doesn't like it to get around when employees are fired for stealing or some other problem like that. Mike Evans wasn't a friend, but he was an okay guy. I found out the company fired him because items he was taking to guests' rooms went missing. He told them he didn't steal anything, but management let him go anyway. What he didn't tell them, because he didn't think they'd believe him, was that Diana was around playing up to him both times guest property went missing." I suppressed a gasp as another of the men in Diana's life was mentioned in connection with a story that didn't end well. Neely glanced at me as she spoke.

"Andi told us Diana was dating a guy by that name."

"That's not surprising, is it?" Mark asked.

"Did he see her lift the items?" Mark shook his head in response to my question.

"No. That was part of the reason he didn't bother to say anything about it. Mostly, he was just relieved he didn't get into more trouble than he did. The laptop and camera and other stolen items were pricey enough to get him charged with a felony." Mark glanced at the menu that featured Mediterranean-themed dishes.

"You've been very helpful. Let us buy you lunch, okay?" Neely asked.

"That would be nice. Thanks. I hope none of this will keep you from opening a shop if that's what you want to do, Tara. Don't let Diana Durand's troubles kill your dream, okay?" I smiled at his earnestness and felt another twinge of guilt. I'd never be good as an undercover cop or a spy.

"I hear you. There are troubled people everywhere, aren't there?"

"You've got that right!" He beamed at me again. "You can't let them stop you!"

What an upbeat, resilient guy, I thought. One of the blessings of youth.

"Do you two want something? I'm going to take my sandwich back with me to the employee break area. You could join me for lunch there."

"I'm full. What about you, Tara?"

"No, Mom. I'm stuffed too." I replied, still playing out my role as Tara Brown.

"We'll walk back with you, though. It would be interesting to hear what Howard Humphrey has to say about Diana Durand. Maybe he'll talk to us."

"I wouldn't count on it. He's big on keeping it 'all in the family' when it comes to talking about whatever went on between him, his uncle, and Diana. That's what he told me when I asked him about Edgar and Diana, along with a request that I 'butt out.' I'll be right back," Mark said as he stepped up to the counter to place his order.

"All in the family, huh? That's an odd way of putting it. Do you think Howard was acting in a protective way toward his uncle or was he still hoping to keep his options open with Diana after she dumped him and cheated on Edgar?" I asked.

"Who knows? He was seen with her after Edgar told her to take a hike. He must have had some sort of unfin-

ished business with her if he wasn't still stuck on her."
Neely shrugged.

"Hmm, that's a good point. I wonder what kind of
unfinished business that could have been." Before Neely
could speculate, Mark was back. She rushed to the cash
register to make good on her offer to pay for his lunch.

"That was fast!" I exclaimed.

"I always order the same thing—gyro with tzatziki
sauce. They started boxing it up for me when I opened the
door. Great food! Great service!"

Once Neely returned after paying Mark's lunch tab, we
headed back to the golf shop. That's when I remembered
another question we had for him about Diana.

"Mark, did Diana have a boyfriend who worked in
security?"

"Not that I'm aware of, but why not? She made friends
easily enough, as you know. Men friends, anyway. Why
do you ask?"

"We heard about Judi Stephenson's situation and
wondered how Diana was able to plant merchandise for
security to find at just the right moment, if that's what
happened. We wondered if a boyfriend in security told her
they were on the way since the visit was intended to be a
surprise."

"I didn't consider that angle. Since you two seem to
know so much about what's gone on around here, it may
not be news to you that she was seeing a guy in management. Dave Winnick's got big dreams and isn't shy about
sharing them with anyone who'll listen. He wants to end
up as CEO of the resort someday and intends to expand
the property. I figured Dave slipped her the information to

avoid a scandal over the fact that he'd been involved with a woman caught stealing from the company he hopes to run someday."

"Would he have been in the loop on an unannounced visit by security?"

"I'm not certain who security reports to when it comes to something like that, but if it involved Diana, he probably got a heads up about it. It wouldn't have been the first time he helped her out."

"We heard she and Winnick let the flame die out once she made a move to cozy up with Edgar."

"Well, I didn't know about Edgar, remember? She did tell me she'd broken it off with Dave. When I asked her why, she said she'd figured out it wasn't a good idea to date your boss."

"It's hard to believe that would matter to Diana," I muttered.

"For me too. I'd be more willing to believe what she figured out is that it's not a good idea to make it obvious that you're dating the boss." Mark nodded in agreement with Neely's point.

"That's an interesting idea. Maybe she was continuing to see him even after she took up with Edgar," I suggested.

"And me, if I hadn't told her to get lost. And maybe Howard. And Mike in Guest Services, until they fired him. Who knows how many other men she was stringing along? Good luck sorting out Diana's messes."

"For a man with big dreams, Dave Winnick wasn't too choosy when it came to women, was he?" I mused.

"Well, like I said, Diana was gorgeous. She loved socializing and could really turn on the charm when she wanted to—quite a trophy wife. When I ran into her that day with Howard's Uncle Edgar, it seemed clear to me that Diana had a different kind of marriage in mind. Why hook up with someone like Winnick and face years of work as a corporate wife when she could marry some guy like Edgar with a short 'use by date' and end up with his money?"

"My, my, you have given this some thought, haven't you?" Neely asked Mark as we found ourselves back at the Blue Haven Pro Shop.

"Too much, I'm afraid," he replied with a grim expression on his face.

I wondered what that meant. He seemed to have come to grips with the kind of woman Diana Durand was and I didn't hear anything in what he said to suggest he still had an ax to grind or bore her the kind of ill demonstrated by the person who strangled her. Still, his comment was a curious one. Unfortunately, didn't have a chance to ask him about it.

When we opened the door and stepped into the store, my mind went blank. Neely and I froze. Detective Miller was standing in front of me, looking around as if he'd just entered the pro shop ahead of us. When he turned to see who'd just entered the store, he spotted me. He did a double-take, glancing at me then Neely and back at me again. I felt trapped as someone entered the shop behind me preventing me from making a quick escape.

"Well, well, well, Miriam Webster, we meet again."

"Hello, Detective." My voice sounded odd, almost squeaky as I acknowledged Hank Miller's greeting. Off to my left, Howard Humphrey went on alert. Out of the corner of my eye, I saw him step behind the counter from a back room. He stood, motionless now, not far from where he'd been when we left earlier with Mark. As his eyes moved from me to the detective, he shoved the papers he held into a large manila envelope.

"Miriam? I thought you said your name was Tara?" Mark asked as he turned to face me. His eyes zeroed in on me in a way that made me squirm. "You're not really interested in opening a bake shop, are you?" Hank Miller looked puzzled. I blushed under their gazes.

Some Mata Hari! My first undercover operation and I'm nabbed, I thought. I glanced at Neely, who was smiling, but didn't appear to be ready to come to my defense with some clever explanation.

"Bake shop? I thought you were writing a script." My heart raced at the sound of Andi Stoeckel's voice as she stepped around from behind me, and stared now, too.

"Hey, Hemingway, is that really you? What are you doing here?" Carl asked, emerging from behind a golf club exhibit.

"Hemingway?" Mark asked almost in a whisper.

"Whoa, you look hot!" Joe bellowed as he popped out from the same location. "Are you on a date with the detective?" Then he took a closer look at Neely. "With a chaperone? Neely, that is you, right? Where's all your hair?"

I felt my face flush again—with embarrassment. I'm not sure what was more mortifying—getting caught sneaking around using a fake name to con people or being asked that question about dating the detective. As I stood there, speechless, I spotted Howard on the move again.

This time he hustled as he headed out from behind the counter and into the back room.

"Very funny, you guys. Nobody's here on a date with or without a chaperone," Neely said in a chiding tone.

"Sorry. Miriam's husband might not find it so funny," Joe apologized.

"He doesn't seem to be around much though, does he? Maybe she figures what he doesn't know won't hurt him. Is that right, *Tara?*" Carl asked with that poker face of his.

"What's going on with the name game, Tara, Miriam, Hemingway—whatever your name really is?" Mark asked.

"I'd like to hear the answer to that, too, if you don't mind." Hank Miller's blue eyes seemed to see right through me.

"So would I!" Andi added.

My mind went blank. My mouth went dry. What could I say? Fortunately, I was saved by the bell when a low ding-dong issued from the back room where Howard had taken refuge. Mark glanced toward the sound, and then took a closer look, this time, at Joe and Carl. His eyes lit up as he spoke.

"Wait a second. You're the guys from Seaview Cottages. I saw you in here talking to Howard a couple of weeks ago. If you were hoping to quiz him the way your friends did me, you just missed your chance. Howard Humphrey has left the building."

Mark's comments got the detective's attention. He turned in time to see Howard Humphrey outside through the large windows behind the checkout counter. Howard was taking big strides and moving at a good clip.

"What's the hurry?" Hank Miller asked in a low voice almost as if he were speaking to himself. "Hang on a second. Don't anyone go anywhere." He stepped away and placed a quick phone call. I presume it had something to do with picking up Howard Humphrey since I heard him say "out the back and heading to the parking lot." When he returned, the detective ignored the rest of us and spoke to Mark Hudson.

"Where were you between midnight and seven a.m. on the morning Diana Durand was killed?"

Shoot! I thought. *We should have asked him that question.* I hoped Mark had a good answer since I hated to believe he was Diana's killer. Instead of answering Hank Miller's question, he posed one of his own. I was surprise that his tone had become belligerent.

"Why don't you ask the woman with multiple names and phony occupations that question? I've had it with being set up by screwy women!"

"As a matter of fact, I've already done that. Ms. Webster's the one who discovered Diana Durand's body on the bluff near Seaview Cottages."

"Really?" Andi asked. "Why were you sneaking around, using a fake name, and asking a bunch of questions as if you had no idea what was going on?"

"Bribing people, too. I'll bet you didn't even bake these, did you?" Mark asked, holding up the little box of scones he still carried.

"Bribery is right. Those are the best scones I've ever eaten. Still, what's the story? Are you a fake baker or a fake scriptwriter?" Andi asked.

Detective Miller's head was moving back and forth as

Andi and Mark pummeled me with questions. It was almost as if he were watching a tennis match. He raised both hands.

"Please, leave the questions to me. I already warned these folks not to do it, so I'm sure no one is here snooping into police business, right?"

Neely shuffled. Carl and Joe did too, much to my surprise. I bowed my head to avoid making eye contact with Hank. That wasn't strictly because I felt embarrassed. There was a tone in his voice I found irritating. Having been nabbed with my hand in the cookie jar now was probably not the time to glare defiantly at the lawman, so I kept my eyes focused firmly on the floor.

"Oh, come on. What harm could there be in asking a few questions?" Joe argued.

"Yeah," Carl echoed him. "If anyone knows who else Diana was dating, it must be Howard. We wanted to know if he spotted her out on the beach with someone since he's renting the old Upton Sinclair place down there."

"He is?" I asked as my head popped up. Joe and Carl both nodded. "Edgar said Howard was staying with him at the Twain Cottage."

"Not every night, obviously," Carl retorted.

"That's good sleuthing," Neely said.

"Thanks," Joe said. "We've got to do what we can to help you ladies since that strangler might have seen you." I opened my mouth to chide him about the use of that term "ladies" given how annoying it sounded. Mainly because Deputy Devers so often paired it with "old" in a derogatory way. Andi piped up before I could utter a syllable.

"Is that true? If you found the body and the killer saw you, why can't you identify the murderer?" Andi asked with alarm and suspicion.

"I can assure you that if we'd spotted the killer we wouldn't be nosing around," I said with conviction. "Diana's murderer has the advantage, I'm afraid. We're almost certain the culprit was nearby when we found Diana's body."

"Wow! That's creepy. No wonder you're here pumping people for info. I'd be trying to find out whodunit, too." Andi shrugged and then appeared as though she had more to say.

Hank had both hands up making those stop motions again. He obviously wasn't happy about Andi's comment and appeared ready to do something drastic. That possibility ratcheted up my already sky-high stress level. Then I recalled the detective's previous threat and fought hard to squelch a nervous giggle. I couldn't do it.

"You'd better watch what you say, Andi, or you'll get hauled off to the hoosegow for promoting interference with the course of justice."

"Hauled off where? For what?" Mark asked in a worried way amid a round of snickers from Joe, Carl, and Neely.

"That's it!" Hank cried. "Get out of here or I will call a paddy wagon and have all of you transported to the hoosegow to spend the night." Mark took a step toward the door.

"Not you," Hank exclaimed in an exasperated tone. Despite his attempt to grouse at us, Hank couldn't keep his upper lip from twitching.

"The rest of you—please leave now. I have a few questions for Mark, here. Then, I promise, I'll help *the ladies*
out by having a chat with Howard Humphrey. I've got
plenty of questions for him."

The detective smirked at me, as if deliberately trying to
annoy me with the emphasis he placed on "the ladies"
when he used that phrase. Two can play that game. I can
be plenty annoying, too.

"Oh, I can vouch for Mark, Detective. He's been
forthcoming and I'm sure he has nothing to hide. Tell him
everything you told me, Mark. Don't leave anything out,
okay?" Mark nodded. Then I smiled my most irritatingly
sweet smile. Hank's brow furrowed as he wearily shook
his head.

"No wonder Devers is the shell of the man he once
was. Go!" Hank commanded, pointing to the door. I
doubt Deputy Devers was ever much more of a man than
he is now, but I didn't contradict the detective. My work
here was done. Almost.

"I'm leaving. I want to apologize for my deception,
Mark and Andi. Let me make it up to you by bringing you
more treats, okay?" Mark nodded but didn't say a word.

"That would be awesome. I'm going now, too. Good
luck, Mark." Andi smiled at him as we left en masse.

"Call Judi. She wants to speak to you," Andi whispered as soon as the door to the pro shop shut behind us. I
nodded.

"How did you know where to find us?" Neely asked.

"You two aren't very sneaky for a couple of sleuths."
Joe and Carl snickered.

"We didn't have much trouble seeing through your

disguises, did we?" Carl asked. Joe chortled. I glared at them and they stopped. Then I sighed. They were right. Andi was, too.

"At least you didn't have to go to much trouble since we apparently left a trail of bread crumbs for you to follow like Hansel and Gretel," I offered.

"Scone crumbs," she replied as she waved goodbye.

15

Murder, Men, and Motives

"WOW! THAT WAS a close one, wasn't it?" Joe asked as we walked to the exit that led from the mall to the parking lot. "The detective was ready to throw the book at us!"

"I doubt it. Hank Miller likes us. I can tell." As she said that, she looked sideways at me. I was on the verge of blushing again and decided to move the conversation in a more worthwhile direction.

"How did you find out about Howard's summer place?" I asked.

"Charly called us," Carl replied.

"Why?" Neely asked.

"She said all her other operatives were on assignment." As Carl said that, he adopted the blank expression he often wore which I now recognized as a cover for his troublemaking.

"Yeah, of course, she did." Carl cracked a smile in response to my sarcasm.

"It was worth a try."

"No fooling around right now, please. Tell us what really happened," Neely insisted.

"Charly called us and said she needed us to go see if Howard Humphrey was at work in the pro shop. If he was there, we were supposed to chat him up—ask him if he'd seen Diana Durand on the beach near where he's renting that cottage—alone or with someone else. Of course, we weren't going to do that without finding out why she wanted us to do it. That's when she told us you all were poking your noses into this whodunit business."

"She didn't say that either."

"Not exactly," Joe admitted. "Something close to it though which is why Carl and I agreed to help you ladies."

"Will you stop with the '*ladies*' bit, please?" I asked. "Are you taking social skills lessons from Deputy Devers?" Both men stared impassively at me now. Maybe they were playing with me again or simply clueless about the concept of social skills. Either way, I let it drop. "Never mind."

"Why weren't you speaking with Howard when we arrived at the shop if you were on assignment for Charly?" Neely asked.

"Howard said he'd be right with us. He was finishing up an inventory or something like that and stepped into the stock room. While we waited, we were looking at the new drivers they carry in the shop—too pricey for most of the golfers that play on the Dunes Course but some fine equipment." Joe swung an imaginary golf club. "Then you two walked in and our plan fell apart."

"I think it was game over before that, don't you? There's no way you two could question Howard Humphrey once Detective Miller walked into the store."

"Good point, Neely," Carl said.

"It all happened so fast," Joe added. "Just like when Howard bugged out of there..." Carl interrupted him.

"Como alma que lleva el diablo, right, Joe?" Carl spoke to us before Joe could reply. "That means 'like a soul fleeing the devil.' Joe's teaching me important Spanish phrases."

"That's pretty good, Carl. In this case, el diablo was Hank Miller. Howard got all agitated when you addressed him as detective," Neely pointed out.

"I noticed."

"Well, if you need us to do anything else, don't hesitate to call. We don't mind being Charly's angels, do we, Joe?"

"Charly's angels. That's a good one, amigo." We stopped at Neely's car as the two men continued to wherever they had parked. By the time Neely was behind the wheel, they were back toot-tooting the horn on the golf cart they'd used to make the trip from Seaview Cottages to the Blue Haven Resort.

It suddenly hit me that the Seaview Cottages community is close enough to the resort that Dave Winnick and his development team might find it irresistible. With a few upgrades, it would be a quick way to expand the resort's holdings. Just when I'd settled on the notion that Diana's death was tied to the way she treated men or the petty scams she was running, I was drawn back to the prospect that there was a bigger game afoot. I shared that possibility with Neely as we settled into her car.

"If the HOA meeting minutes are correct, the community leadership already ran 'Big Blue' off once. What if Mark's got it right about Dave Winick's ambitions? He could be skulking around our property because he's figured out some way to get his grasping hands on Seaview Cottages and expand the empire he plans to rule one day." Neely backed out of the parking place and headed to the parking lot exit before she responded to my comment.

"If he's back after the HOA Board members flat out rejected Blue Haven Resort's recent offer, I wouldn't be shocked if his next attempt was an underhanded one. That's assuming he's not a wonton strangler looking for another neck to wring, right?" I shuddered at Neely's words.

"The two possibilities aren't mutually exclusive, are they?" I paused. "In fact, if Diana got wind that a big deal is in the works, there'd be lots more money at stake than the thousands she was stealing from Edgar or the Blue Moon Boutique." Neely nodded as she turned onto the roadway leading back to Seaview Cottages.

"I'm sure Diana would have found that kind of money irresistible," Neely suggested.

"I agree. It's also the kind of money that could have gotten a troublesome woman like Diana killed," I added.

"By spilling the beans to Edgar and making a tidy sum for herself on the side, you mean?" Neely asked.

"Yes. If Edgar had taken her up on the offer, a leak like that could have killed the deal. Or worse, if Dave Winick's no longer playing by the rules. If the information she wanted to sell to Edgar exposed unethical or even criminal behavior on Winick's part, that would have given him a motive for murder."

"I hear you, Miriam. Dave Winick put up with a surprising amount of trouble from her, but I can't imagine he'd let her get him sent to prison. Let's say he's back circling us like a shark because he smells blood in the water given our community's money problems. Are you suggesting he's courting Greta Bishop to entice her into voting his way?"

"Yes, although it would take more than that. He needs more than Greta's support. Seaview Cottages has money problems, but we're not in default on loans or payment of back taxes or anything that would force us into receivership."

"Who has access to the accounts you've been reviewing? Could a lovesick member of the Executive Committee, like Greta, allow Winick to get his hands on the Seaview Cottages accounts? Has anyone monkeyed around with the books?"

"I haven't done an audit, but we could ask for one if we want to verify that there are receipts for the money that's been spent since the last official audit was done." I paused wondering if I was going off the deep end because, in hindsight, I should have been more vigilant about my personal financial affairs. "When I went back over expenditures for the past few years, nothing jumped out at me as unusual this year. Greta's one of the people who can sign checks or move money from reserves into a checking account on behalf of the HOA. There must be a rule on the books about how large a sum she can spend or reallocate without authorization from the Finance Committee or other members of the Executive Committee. These are great questions. I'll go over the rules and see what I can find out."

"Maybe we need to go back to Edgar and quiz him

again about the information Diana wanted to sell him. He may know something he doesn't realize he knows—that's often how our minds work. You can bet Charly's working on the big swindle angle already, though. Let's finish our work for the day, and then have a debriefing session this evening." I nodded enthusiastically at Neely's idea.

"My house, okay? Believe it or not, I still have scones left. I kind of got carried away."

"Let's do it. We'll order takeout from Chef Tony, and no one will have to cook a thing." Neely said. "Why don't we park in the beach lot rather than going all the way home? It'll be quicker than driving home, first, and then walking back to the old Sinclair Cottage and other beachside homes. We've got plenty of walking to do once we start making the rounds. There's a cluster of older places that used to be part of the original Writers' Circle. They're not far from the beach lot. After that, we'll have a bit of a hike to visit those that are more far flung."

"That makes sense. We should probably walk the entire route from the cottages to Fitzgerald's Bluff. I imagine the police investigators have done that already, but maybe they missed something that might explain what happened the morning Diana was strangled." I looked down at my feet and sighed. "It's a good thing our undercover disguises include sensible shoes."

"I don't own any other kind, do you? I never was a fan of stilettos even bef0re I gave up on high heels altogether years ago. We'll get our exercise in for the day if we walk all the way to Fitzgerald's Bluff. We don't want to miss a clue if there is one, do we?" Then, Neely whacked the steering wheel excitedly. "You know what? You should write about this mystery, Miriam. It doesn't have to be 'true crime' if you don't want to detail all the criminal procedures and gross tidbits from the autopsy report or crime lab. If you take up the pen, you'd be our first writer in residence."

"Ha! *Of Murder, Men, and Motives*—an epic tale by Miriam Webster. If I take up the pen, it'll require more guts than I've exhibited so far." That comment wasn't only about my untested talent as a writer or the fact that the mystery of Diana's death remained unsolved. I was worrying about the mysteries in my own life that I haven't had the courage to tackle openly either.

Neely glanced at me as she drove, perhaps wondering what I meant by my lack of guts or my sudden silence. She didn't prod. In fact, she had another suggestion altogether.

"While I'm driving, why don't you give Judi Stephenson a call and find out what she wants to tell you."

"Okay, I ought to be able to reach her in Duneville Downs since we're not still on the road and not down in among the dunes."

"This close to the resort, you'll have plenty of bars on your phone. Blue Haven Resort doesn't want to inconvenience its guests."

Neely was right, of course. My phone call went through instantly and Judi Stephenson picked up on the first ring. When I told her who was calling, I used the name Tara, at first, and then quickly added that my real name was Miriam Webster. Before I could explain further, she interrupted me.

"Andi told me all about it," she said in a terse, irritated tone. "I should hang up on you, but I won't because I hope you'll get to the bottom of the sleazy business Diana Durand was involved in. That includes the thefts that got me fired. I don't want that stupid job back, but I'd like to have my name cleared and a letter of apology from Blue Haven Resort management in case the matter comes up again."

"Believe me, I'm as eager as you are to find out what happened. One question I have for you is what merchandise the security team found in your drawer. We're trying to understand how big a scam Diana was running."

"That's easy—it's burned into my memory by the horror and humiliation I felt. They found an entire box of those hand painted silk scarves—each one individually wrapped as they are before we put them out on display at a couple hundred dollars each. The box was shoved inside one of those large, ridiculously overpriced designer totes as if I planned to walk out of there with the thing in my hand. There were half a dozen pieces of costume jewelry wrapped in tissue paper and stuffed inside the bag, too. I'd say the haul that day would have been close to three thousand dollars retail."

"Wow!" I exclaimed. "Not bad for a day's work. I wonder how she planned to get it out of there."

"Well, she might have been able to walk out of there. No one would have thought it was odd for her to carry such an expensive bag. Or she could have planned to pass it off to one of her men friends who stopped by. I don't like accusing anyone after what I've been through, but that big guy, Boo, often carried a backpack that was large enough to stash the merchandise I'm describing to you. I'm even more hesitant to accuse a coworker, which is why I wanted to speak to you rather than relay information through Andi. Diana had a parade of men come through the shop who worked at the resort, including her golf instructor and his boss. Both men visited her several times while I was in the shop. Maybe one of them was her partner in crime that day. I don't know. It still makes me sick to think about it. She ruined my life. I won't say that I'm happy she's dead, but I'm not all that sad, either."

The bitterness in her voice was understandable, but still shocking. She went back on the list along with Dave Winick as a person who could have wanted revenge against Diana. *Of Murder, Men, and Motives* was going to be a long work of fiction if we didn't start cutting down on the number of suspects soon. The men she'd mentioned were on it, too.

"Okay, so the mysterious man with scars and tattoos you're calling Boo, Mark Hudson, and Howard Humphrey are the men you're talking about, right?"

"Yes. If you already know the men I'm referring to, you've been doing your homework. Please don't let it get back to Boo that I sicced you on him. He's scary. Not just the way he looks, but he's eerily quiet. Sometimes, I didn't hear him come in or leave—but I knew he'd been through the store because I'd catch a whiff of his cologne in the air." I sat up straighter. A little shiver passed through me. I hadn't seen Boo, but from his description, the idea that he could have been the person lurking nearby when Domino and I discovered Diana's body was creepier than spotting Dave Winick spying on us.

"Cologne? What cologne?" I asked, anxiously. Neely wavered a little on the road and I instinctively reached for the steering wheel. She slapped my hand lightly, steadied the car, and drove on while I picked up the conversation with Judi.

"I don't know. Some cologne Diana said she bought for him. Stole, is probably more like it. If not out and out theft like she was doing at the boutique, then a dirty trick like the one she pulled on Howard Humphrey's uncle Edgar. I couldn't believe it when I found out she'd traded in the newer model for a much older one until she started droning on and on about Edgar's money. From the way she talked, Edgar Humphrey was her personal ATM."

"How did Howard take being tossed aside for his rich uncle?"

"I'm not sure since he's almost as quiet as Boo. Howard kept creeping around even after she dumped him. And even after his uncle dumped her, which I found weird. That's one reason I wonder now if he was more than a simpering idiot mooning over her and was helping Diana rip off the boutique."

"I understand. How about the other men involved with Diana? Not just Boo or Mark Hudson. Did you ever see any of them object to being kicked to the curb as she moved from one guy to another?"

"She came here griping one day about Mark Hudson telling her off for sneaking around behind Edgar's back. She was the one who was angry, not Mark. He might have been the first guy who really called it quits with Diana. Even Dave Winnick kept crawling back."

"He did?" I asked. "Does that mean Dave and Diana were still involved romantically after she started seeing Edgar?" The car weaved again, ever so slightly, as Neely shifted in her seat when she heard me ask that question.

"Truthfully, I don't know what they were doing. I almost bumped into them on my way to the parking lot. They were standing just outside the exit from the mall area only a few inches apart, speaking intently about something. I assumed it was romantic, but I can't say that for sure. It was an awkward moment when they realized I'd spotted them. Diana sort of glared at me. Maybe that's how I became the lucky winner of the get Diana out of jail card, and she picked me as the coworker to set up."

"Hmm. That's not a bad idea, Judi. Especially, if she thought you were eavesdropping and overheard them discussing something you weren't supposed to hear."

"I wish I had heard something. A little leverage might have given me a chance to bargain my way out of losing my job. Maybe I wasn't supposed to see them together that way. As shrewd as Diana was, don't you think she would have been afraid to target me if she thought I had information I could use?"

"As in blackmail, you mean?" Neely's grip on the wheel didn't wobble this time, but she glanced at me, taking her eyes off the road for a split second. I was beginning to wonder if I should have waited until we were safely parked in the beach lot before calling Judi Stephenson.

"Exactly. That's what Diana would have done if she'd come up with even a scrap of information she could use to manipulate someone. Am I right?"

"Yes," I said as the wheels in my head went around and around, adding another motive for murder to the list. Maybe Diana had tried to get the owner to buy back the information she'd attempted to peddle to Edgar and the person she tried to blackmail objected. "This conversation has been very interesting. Useful, too. I appreciate your willingness to talk to me."

"No problem," she sighed. "You probably won't be surprised to hear that the police have contacted me."

"Hey, they've had a couple of conversations with me already."

"Lucky you. Andi told me you found Diana's body on Fitzgerald's Bluff. That had to be uncomfortable, to say the least. Have the police made any progress in finding her killer?"

"I found it more than uncomfortable, Judi. As far as the progress they're making, the lead investigator has made it quite clear that he doesn't see me as a person with whom to discuss the case or share information."

I'm not sure why, but the conversation had started to make me feel more than a little uncomfortable. As a wave of paranoia swept over me, I wondered if she was asking for information about the police investigation to find out what they had on her. I took a deep breath. Nothing in her question had suggested that's what she had in mind, although there was an apprehensive tone in her voice. Before I spoke again, I considered the circumstances in which the police would be interviewing Judi.

"This all has to be very hard for you. Just share the same information with them that you gave me. It's quite enlightening. They'll have an even better idea than I do about how to use it."

"Sure. Stay safe. It's not always a good thing to get mixed up in other people's messes, is it? Bye." With that,

Judi Stephenson ended the call.

"Did you catch all that?"

"Most of it," Neely replied as she slowed and flipped on her left turn signal. Seconds later, Neely turned into the Old Cottage Beach lot and found a parking place right away. I had expected the lot and the beach to be busier given that it was a gorgeous day and the summer people had started to arrive.

As Neely explained when I expressed my surprise, except on weekends, the lot was mostly used by local people picking up or dropping off their kids at the Blue Haven Bluejackets Summer Camp on our left. The resort had a shuttle for the children of hotel guests, some of whom participated in the overnight camp program, staying at a well-appointed lodge that was nothing like the bunkrooms for kids at typical camps.

"The point of renting a beach cottage for the summer is so you don't have to drive to the beach and park in the lot since you're living there already." I nodded. That's one of the things I enjoy about the location of our community. We have a small pedestrian walkway that takes us over the roadway, so we don't have to deal with traffic even when there's a special event at the resort.

"Where's the cottage Howard Humphrey's renting?" I asked wondering once again about his relationship with Diana after what Judi had said. The image of his hasty retreat from golf shop also popped into mind. Where was he? Had he gone back to his cottage or had the police caught up with him and taken him in for questioning? Hank Miller didn't strike me as the sort of man you could run from for long.

For some reason, that thought suddenly made me feel like blushing again. Neely eyed me as if she could read something in my body language. I launched into an account of my call with Judi and eventually ended back at the point where I wondered, aloud this time, if Howard was in his cottage.

"The old Sinclair Cottage is one of the first places we'll run into that sits outside the cluster of summer places." Neely pointed to a mishmash of structures in various sizes and trimmed in an array of bright colors. "That call to Judi points in lots of different directions doesn't it? Not just different men, but motives, too."

"It sure does. I wonder what Midge and Marty found out about Diana's last breakfast—where she was and, if she had someone with her, who was it? That ought to help steer us one way or another when it comes to narrowing down suspects and motives. I'm getting a headache from intracranial whiplash as I switch directions about whodunit so fast."

"Ooh, 'intracranial whiplash.' That's great. Make sure you use that in your story, *Murder on Fitzgerald's Bluff.*"

"I like that title much better than the one I suggested, Neely! I might just steal it, or something like it, if I decide to write about this mystery," I said. "It's too bad we're moving so slowly. At this point, there's still not much of a story to tell, is there? Maybe we'll get closer to understanding what's going on when we meet for dinner."

"We don't have to put off all the debriefing until then. Midge and Marty will be here soon, and we'll have to decide who's going to visit which beach houses. They'll update us when they show up. Let's see what surprises

they have for us. We have more than a few for them."
With that, Neely and I slid out of our seats, stepped into
the sea breeze, and found ourselves facing a new surprise.
This one did not come from Midge and Marty.

16

The Blue Haven Bluejackets

W E HADN'T WALKED more than a few feet from our car when I noticed a group of boys near the entrance to the camp dressed in t-shirts that said Blue Haven Bluejackets on them. They were dashing about, running in and out of bushes and trees near the open gates along a gravel road that led into the camp. Those bushes and trees bore the recognizable mark of the landscaping used at the resort. The Blue Haven Resort logo was etched along with the camp's name above the entrance. What caught my eye was the fact that several of the boys were tugging at a scarf.

"Look at that, Neely."

"They've got a game of Capture the Flag in progress— or maybe it's just about over since a couple of the boys seem to have the flag in hand."

"They may be using it as a flag for their game, but that's a scarf. Isn't the design familiar to you?"

"Well, I'll be a monkey's uncle!" Neely took off toward the group of a dozen boys. "Yoo-hoo! Can you boys help me please?" They stopped whatever wrangling they'd been doing and stared at her.

"Are you lost?" One of them called out.

"No. But you may have something I lost. That looks like a scarf I'm missing." Most of the boys backed off when they heard Neely's reply. Apparently, it was game over. They didn't exactly run for it, but stepped away and left the two boys holding the flag to face us by themselves.

"It does?" The older of the two boys asked.

"Yes. I'm Neely, what's your name?"

"Brandon. This is my brother, Nathan. Nice to meet you."

"It's nice to meet you, too. This is my friend, Miriam."

"Hey," Brandon said, acknowledging my presence. "Where did you say you lost your scarf?"

"She didn't say," I replied. I wondered why that mattered to him. In the condition the scarf was in, he couldn't be concerned about its value. Maybe he thought Neely was going to give them grief about what he and his brother, and their friends had done to it. "You're not in any trouble no matter where you found it."

"I'm not worried about that. I am wondering if I should call the police since you don't look anything like the lady we saw running on the beach that morning who lost the scarf."

"Woman?" I asked.

"Running—as in jogging?" Neely added.

"Nah. She and some guy were fooling around—laughing and splashing in the water," Brandon explained.

"They were celebrating," Nathan added.

"That's what she told us when we picked up the scarf for her. She told us to keep it," Brandon said.

"Plus, she said she had lots more of them. Remember?"

Brandon nodded when Nathan asked him that question.

"This means you're lying, Neely—if that's a real name. That's why I'm pretty sure we should call the police." The two boys moved a little closer together but stared at us defiantly.

"Yeah, also because we heard she's dead," Nathan whispered.

"That's true. We already know that since my dog and I found her a little while later. I'm certain we should call the police," I said, pulling my phone out to make the call. Neely made eye contact and nodded in agreement. "The police need to hear what you've just told us as soon as possible." For the first time, the two boys appeared as if they might bolt.

"Don't get cold feet, guys. Talking to the police is the right idea. Nobody's going to cause you any trouble since you haven't done anything wrong," Neely said in a reassuring tone.

"That's what you think. We weren't supposed to be out there in the dunes on our own that early in the morning. When our parents hear we sneaked out of the camp, we're toast!" I didn't tell them, but angry parents were the least of their worries. As I dug out Hank Miller's card that I'd tossed into my purse, I was concerned that the man who'd been on the beach with Diana might be interested in tracking down the boys who'd seen him that morning.

"What did the guy with her look like?" I asked as I typed in the detective's phone number and hit the call button. I held my breath, prepared for them to tell me about a big, scary-looking man.

"Ordinary." Before I could ask Brandon what he meant by that, the detective answered my call. I was a bit surprised since I expected to get his voice mail.

"Hank Miller speaking," he said in the clipped tones of a busy man.

"Uh, Detective, this is Miriam Webster. Are you still at the resort?"

"Yes. Why?"

"We have two people with important information who need to speak to you right away."

"I'm in the middle of something—can you have them meet me at the police station in Duneville Downs in an hour or so?"

"No. I don't believe they can drive." Both boys looked at me as if I was crazy and shook their heads no. "I'm not sure their parents would want them to get into a car with Neely and me, either." I put the phone against my chest for a second, so the detective couldn't hear the question I asked the boys.

"Are your parents staying at the resort?" That got two nods and two expressions of dread.

"Hank, I'm going to put Brandon on the phone and let you speak directly to him. I presume his parents will want to be with him when you question him. You don't want to put that off for long, though." Then I turned away from the boys and spoke to Hank Miller in a low voice. "They were here at the beach, yesterday. It was very early in the morning and they ran into Diana with some 'ordinary' looking man. They have her scarf."

"As in our murder weapon?" Hank asked.

"No, thank goodness. She dropped this one on the

beach before..." I stopped that sentence not able to use words like strangled or murdered with the boys nearby. "...she died."

"Okay. Let me speak to him. If he gives me his parents' names and their room number at the resort hotel, I'll contact them and have them accompany me to hear what they have to say."

"I know you'll tell their parents what an important contribution they're making to a police investigation. You don't want your key informants to get into any trouble with their parents, right?"

"Uh, I'll try. Are you all in a safe place?" I looked around, suddenly feeling terribly conspicuous. Hank's mind must have moved down the same track that had convinced me to call him right away. He needed to act quickly to find out what Nathan and Brandon had witnessed and protect them.

"Not exactly." I explained where we were, but not why. "We can wait for you in Neely's navy-blue hatchback parked in the beach lot, okay?" Brandon and Nathan both shuffled their feet as if they might be thinking once again about making a break for the campgrounds. Just as they did that, I heard a horn toot. Neely and I turned and waved at Midge and Marty in a cherry red Mustang convertible.

"Woohoo! Look at that cool car!" Nathan exclaimed.

"Hank, will you make that Midge Gaylord's car instead, okay?" I quickly told him how to spot the car now parked next to Neely's hatchback.

"Here you go," I said, handing my phone to Brandon. "Detective Hank Miller needs to speak to you, but he has to contact your parents first. You heard the message I gave him about what to tell your parents. There's no way you two are going to be toast, okay?" That coaxed a smile from both boys—more from relief than happiness.

"Hello," Brandon said as soon as he took the phone. Before he could add anything else, Nathan spoke up.

"Brandon, tell him about this, too, okay?" Brandon nodded as Nathan pulled a cell phone from the pocket of his shorts and handed it to me.

"Detective, just to be sure we get off on the right foot, you should know that we have the dead lady's phone." Midge and Marty had joined us just in time to hear that news. They let out audible sounds of surprise along with Neely and me.

"Midge and Marty, meet star witnesses, Nathan and Brandon," I said. Brandon nodded, but kept talking to Hank Miller.

"Brandon's on the phone with Detective Miller, who's down the road a bit at the Blue Haven Resort where we ran into him earlier," Neely explained.

"Okay, but what's this about Diana's phone?" Midge asked, getting right to the point.

"We found it. Later," Nathan said. "It was just lying out there in the sand. We figured it fell out of her pocket when she was running around with that Howie guy." My mouth fell open.

"Howie?" I asked. "You know his name?"

"That's what the woman called him," Nathan replied, shrugging his shoulders as if it was no big thing.

"Hang on a second, okay?"

"Why not? I'm not going anywhere, am I?" He asked

and then smiled broadly.

"Brandon, please tell Hank I need to speak to him again before he hangs up." He nodded.

"Well, that beats the heck out of our big news," Marty sighed. "Howard Humphrey was Diana's breakfast companion." Midge jumped in to explain in an excited tone.

"Doward Wilson told us it wasn't the first time the two of them had been in the diner at the truck stop for a late-night snack or crack of dawn breakfast. He figured they'd been partying all night and stopped in for coffee to sober up."

"It was more than that though," Marty added. "According to Diana, they needed a big breakfast because they were facing a long trip and wouldn't get decent food on the plane."

"Brandon and Nathan said they were celebrating when they ran into them on the beach that morning. Did he say what they were celebrating or where they were going?"

"No. They must have had a place nearby where they had their suitcases stashed. Maybe we can answer those questions if we figure out where they were staying or can track Howard down and ask him," Midge said.

"I'm not sure Howard wants to be found, but the police are looking for him. We were going to check on a cottage he's renting when we made the rounds of the summer cottages here. I'm not sure we need to do that, now." I was about to fill them in on the details about the news Joe and Carl had delivered earlier about Sinclair Cottage, and about Howard Humphrey's sudden departure from the pro shop. When Brandon stepped toward us and handed me the phone, I asked Neely to do it instead.

"He's ready to talk to you now."

"Thanks, Brandon," I said as I grabbed the phone.

"It's me again, Hank. I hope you'll ask Howard Humphrey what he was doing with Diana Durand on the beach when he was supposedly at his uncle's house. Brandon must have confirmed what he told us—that he and Nathan heard Diana call the man she was with, Howie. You'll put him on the spot, right?"

"When we catch up to him, we sure will."

"Since you don't have your hands on him already, you should have someone watching for him at the nearby airports," I said and told him what Midge and Marty had learned from speaking to Doward Wilson. Not just that the two of them were out for breakfast together the morning Diana was murdered, but mentioned that they were about to leave for a trip somewhere that involved a long plane flight.

"You all have been busy, haven't you? Until we catch up with this guy, no more poking around!" Issued as an ultimatum, I didn't argue, but I replied curtly.

"Sure, it's already been a long day. I need to go home and liberate Domino. She's been cooped up since I left early this morning."

"Go home. Take care of the dog. That's perfect." I was about to hang up when he spoke again. "Did the boys use that phone?" I blinked a couple of times trying to understand what he was asking. Then it hit me.

"Diana's ghost, huh?"

"Yes."

"Let me ask." The boys had wandered away to get a

closer look at Midge's Mustang. I cupped the phone as I called out to the boys.

"Nathan, Brandon, did you make calls on the cell phone?" They took a few shuffling steps back toward me and glanced at each other warily. "It's okay, you can tell me. You're not in any trouble."

"Yes. Nothing personal or anything like that. When we got back to the camp, we tried to find someone who could tell her that we had her phone," Nathan responded.

"We checked her profile and found her name," Brandon added. "Then we went to her speed dial numbers and called 'Daddy,' but he didn't answer. There was a weird voicemail message, so we didn't say anything."

"Weird, how?"

"Well the guy on the voicemail said his name was Edgar, but his voice sounded a lot like that Howie guy. It was confusing."

"We weren't sure what to do next because right after that our friends, Carter and Kevin, told us there was a dead woman on the beach at Blue Haven. We looked up the story and saw it was that same woman, even if it wasn't the same beach."

"Why didn't you call the police?" Midge asked. They scuffed their feet and looked down at the blacktop without answering her question.

"They didn't want to be 'toast,' right?" Both boys bobbed their heads in agreement with me. I could hear Hank Miller saying something.

"What was that about toast?" He asked.

"Nothing important. The short answer to your question is that the boys called Edgar trying to reach someone who could tell Diana they found her phone. The mystery of Diana's ghostly call from the grave is solved. Once you take them someplace safe and go over all the details with them, they may remember even more. You'll be here soon, won't you?" I suddenly felt anxious for the two brothers. They were doing their best to be brave despite finding themselves involved in a murder investigation and in possession of the dead woman's phone. Of course, in true teen fashion, parental sanctions topped the list as their biggest fear.

"Yes. We've located the parents. I'm going to speak to them now." That sounded like yet another abrupt end to a conversation, but I was wrong. "I shouldn't do anything to encourage you and your active adult companions to get into more trouble, but you handled this well, Miriam." I was floored! It took me a long pause before I could utter a reply.

"Thanks. I'll share that with my gang of old ladies." He laughed as he said goodbye. When I turned to tell the others that Hank had actually paid us a compliment, I froze. My heart rate sped up as I strained to make out the figure of a man. When I blinked, he was gone.

17

The Man Who's *Not* on the Bridge

FROM WHERE I stood in the parking lot, I could see the arched bridge that crosses the road from Seaview Cottages to the dunes and beach quite clearly. I could have sworn someone was standing on the bridge, peering at us. At this distance, I might not have even noticed except that the figure moved for an instant when I turned around and faced the bridge. I squinted, wondering if I needed real glasses since I couldn't see anyone on the bridge now.

"Share what?" Neely asked.

"I'll tell you, but let's get into the cars while we wait for Hank, okay?" My request was made with renewed urgency when I saw movement on the bridge again. The tall man I glimpsed disappeared almost immediately as he strode toward the beach. I stepped closer to Midge and spoke in a low voice as Marty ushered the boys to the Mustang.

"I don't want to scare the boys, but you should put the top up. Turn the engine on and use the AC if it gets too hot, but keep the windows rolled up and the doors locked until Hank gets here." Midge didn't ask why as she dashed to the driver's side of her car. Neely had leaned in to hear me and questioned me quietly.

"That's not funny, so why were you laughing?"

"No, it's not! I'll tell you what Hank said later. Right now, I'm more concerned about the man who's on the bridge."

"Why?" Neely asked as she pushed the glasses up on her nose and frowned as if that would allow her to see all the way to the bridge. "You know my distance vision is no good, but I don't see anyone on the bridge."

"To be more precise, what I should have said is that I'm more concerned about the man who's NOT on the bridge." With that, I called Hank again. When the call went to voice mail, I asked him to please hurry as I slipped into the passenger seat of Neely's car and locked the door.

If Boo was on his way, it would take him ten or fifteen minutes to reach us, even if he moved at a fast clip. I scanned the area around us, searching for a bluff nearby that could give me a higher elevation and a better view of anyone approaching us on foot. When I reached for the door handle to get out of the car, Neely stopped me.

"You're not going anywhere, Miriam Webster!" She was correct, of course. What would I do if I did see the big galoot except run right back to the car. "You haven't even told me why you're so spooked. Spill it!"

"Okay," I responded hoping not to infect her with my panic. I told her what I thought I'd seen, taking in great gulps of air and almost hyperventilating as I uttered Boo's name. I'd never seen or met Boo, but I knew enough about Diana Durand not to unquestionably accept the claim she'd made to Andi that he was a "marshmallow." The car suddenly felt claustrophobic—more like a trap than a haven.

Neely didn't say anything, but by the time I finished, she was also gazing anxiously at the bluffs and beach. She searched behind us too, using her rearview mirror. Midge and Marty appeared to be engaged in an animated conversation with Brandon and Nathan. Thankfully, they didn't seem to be scared or worried in the least.

Neely and I both let out audible sighs of relief when sirens sounded a few minutes later. Not long after that, Hank pulled up behind us. He didn't bother to park before he hopped out of his car. A patrol car pulled up behind him.

"Everyone okay?" Hank shouted. Neely had unlocked the car doors as soon as the sirens closed in on us. I opened my door and slipped out quickly.

"We're all fine now," I replied, almost running toward him until I realized Hank had his gun drawn. When I stopped abruptly, he stowed the gun in a shoulder holster worn under his jacket.

"What was the 'hurry up' message about?" Before I could respond, the doors on Midge's car doors flew open and the boys sprang from the back seat.

"Mom! Dad!" they cried as they rushed into the out-stretched arms of their parents who'd disembarked from the back seat of the patrol car. As the family members embraced and chattered, I told Hank about Boo. After a round of "Boo who?" which evoked a snicker from Neely who'd joined us, Hank was on the phone with a dispatcher. He relayed the description I'd given him of the man and asked for someone to patrol the beach on foot to locate him.

"He sure sounds like the guy *The* Gardeners saw arguing with Diana Durand in the parking lot. Do you want to
tell me how you found out they call him Boo? The short
version, please."

"Sure," I replied. "There isn't that much to tell." Hank
listened intently, his pale blue eyes never wavering from
my face as I explained what we'd learned about him—
including the "marshmallow" bit.

"Well, if he was headed this way, my guess is the sirens
changed his mind." I nodded in response to Hank's
observation as he put his phone away.

"I'm sure you're right. He's probably taken off in the
opposite direction by now."

"We'll have someone waiting for him if he gets as far
as Dickens' Dune or the parking lot near there. Maybe
that's where he was going all along. He could have left a
car parked there," Hank added.

"I also wouldn't be too surprised if he tried to make
his escape using the bridge again. He could have parked at
the Clubhouse. Security at the guard gate would have let
him into the community if he'd made a lunch reservation
or arranged to play a round of golf."

"I doubt he made a reservation for lunch or golf using
'Boo' as his name," Hank murmured.

"I'm sorry we don't have his real name," Neely offered.

"And I apologize if I've got it all wrong and panicked
for no reason when I glimpsed an enormous man with
almost no hair on the bridge. I can't be sure it was him, so
I may have just sicced you on some poor guy trying to
relax at the beach."

"There can't be too many guys around here who fit the description we have for Boo," Neely added.

"Deputy Devers is on patrol in Seaview Cottages. He's supposed to be keeping an eye out for any of our suspects if they turn up."

"Yeah, well, I wouldn't hold your breath waiting for him to get his man," Neely muttered. "Does he even know he's supposed to be looking for Boo?"

"He does now," Hank replied. "It's better to be safe than sorry, Miriam. The guy sounds like he stands out, even at a distance, so you made the right call to send the alert to me." Hank smiled through the stress on his face.

"I doubt I could have stopped myself. My reaction was immediate. It wasn't just that he fit Boo's description, but he also appeared to be watching us from the bridge. I wondered if he'd spotted us at the resort and was waiting for us to return to Seaview Cottages. Then, when he crossed the bridge to the beach, I got worried he'd seen us speaking to the boys and had decided to come after them." I dropped my voice when I mentioned my concern about the boys, even though we were huddled together trying to stay out of earshot of the others.

"If nothing else, once I picked up your message to hurry, it got the boys' parents motivated. Let's hear what our witnesses have to say so we can all get out of here."

When Hank smiled this time, the smile was broader, and the sparkle had returned to his eyes. My heart began to pound again as he gazed at me. He wasn't more than a few inches away. There was something conspiratorial, even intimate, about the connection we'd made as we spoke about the latest twist.

"You're right," I said, my throat dry and my voice a little thin as I took a step toward the boys and their parents. Neely had joined Midge and Marty and introduced herself.

"Brandon and Nathan are incredibly observant and have plenty to say if you can keep them safe. They may be a little too clever for their own good." Hank smirked at my comment. I hustled to say hello to the boys' parents before he had a chance to say "look who's talking" or anything remotely like that.

Even though we no longer made the rounds of the summer cottages, it was another hour before Neely dropped me off at home. I couldn't wait to get inside, change out of the tight jeans I'd worn all day, and slip into my comfortable sweat pants.

I waved goodbye to Neely from my front porch and then unlocked the door. As I did that, I heard Domino woof at me from inside. When I opened the door, Domino jumped up, put her weight against the door, and shut it!

"Domino! It's me, Momma." She ran to the picture window and looked at me from inside. As she did that, I pulled the wig off and mussed up my hair. Domino jumped with joy and spun around. I opened the door and this time she let me in. With or without Domino, I usually come and go from the garage, so maybe coming to the front door in that wig had spooked her.

"What is it, girl? Didn't you recognize me? You saw me leave the house in this silly outfit." I put my bag down and bent down to make eye contact with Domino. I got a big smooch for my effort. Then she went nuts again.

Domino ran from the foyer where I stood, down the

short hallway, and dashed into the kitchen. I heard her make pawing sounds from what must have been the laundry room. Before I could make sense of her odd behavior, she came galloping back. She stood in front of me, bowed as though she wanted to play, and then ran toward the kitchen again. She paused and woofed at me. I took that to mean I was supposed to follow.

"I don't know what you're up to, Domino, but I'm coming." When I got to the kitchen, I could see into the laundry room and stopped. The laundry basket that had been empty when I left this morning was full—piled high with clothes and other items that Domino must have collected from around the house.

"Domino is this a new game, or have you had a major anxiety attack?" I asked her in a weary, annoyed tone.

I dragged myself into the laundry room to take a closer look at what she'd done. A throw I leave at the foot of the bed for Domino to sleep on was the biggest item and sat on top of the pile. I pulled it off and threw it into the washer. Then I began removing slippers and magazines and newspapers and finally got to the bottom. On any ordinary day, Domino collects our mail from the floor in the foyer after it's dropped through the slot in the front door. Then she deposits it in a tray on the coffee table. Today, it was at the bottom of the laundry basket. When I picked it up, I immediately dropped it again.

18

Domino's Game

"**N**O WONDER YOU'RE upset, Domino! I'm so sorry I didn't understand." I picked up the nearly empty laundry basket and put it on the dining table in the kitchen. I was so creeped out that it took me a few more seconds to decide what to do next.

Then, I almost ran to the foyer where I'd dropped my bag on a table near the front door. Once I dug out my phone, I called Charly. Domino and I wandered back toward the kitchen as I waited anxiously for her to answer.

"Hello," she said on the third ring.

"Charly, it's Miriam. I need your advice. Someone has left me something in an envelope with my name scrawled on it. What should I do?" I cleared my voice before going on. "It reeks of the same cologne I smelled when we found Diana's body."

"Call Hank. I'll be right there."

"He might not be happy to hear from me again so soon." I explained how we'd spent that last hour or so at the beach. Our conversation with Hank had ended with yet another warning about the need to stay out of an ongoing murder investigation. Now I was probably in for an "I told you so moment" with him.

"Trust me, Miriam, he's going to want to see what's in that envelope. It's better if he opens it rather than you. There's less chance that you'll contaminate it and he can begin to document what the police refer to as the chain of custody that's important to the collection of evidence."

"I'm afraid the chain has a weak link in it already. There's probably doggy spit to go with the teeth marks Domino left on it. Apparently, it was delivered along with the rest of the morning mail, or soon after. Domino buried it all at the bottom of a laundry basket. She didn't approve of someone dropping the stinky thing through the mail slot into our house."

"That's okay. Domino was doing her best to protect you. If you're right about the scent, it must be paired for her with all the stress and excitement that went on when we found Diana's body. Dogs are incredibly sensitive creatures—Domino, in particular. Call Hank. I'm on my way and I'll bring Emily with me."

"Thanks so much. Domino will be happy to see you and Emily." Domino had been watching me intently with her brow furrowed. When I mentioned Emily's name, her tail began to wag. As soon as I ended the call, I set my phone down and gave Domino the love she deserved for making such a valiant effort to keep bad things away from us.

"You deserve a treat," I said as I found the detective's phone number by going through the recent calls I'd made and redialed it. Domino was almost back to normal as she wolfed down a doggie biscuit. I wish I could say the same about myself. I tried to calm down as I called the detective.

"Hank Miller speaking."

"Uh, Hank. Detective Miller, it's me again—Miriam."

"Hello, Miriam. What's up?" I could almost hear him add "now" to that question, but he restrained himself.

"Charly told me to call you to come get new evidence left here at my home while I was away. Domino got to it first, so it's been worked over a little." I did my best to sound coherent as I filled him in about what I meant by that: describing the item, how it must have turned up inside my house, and Domino's game she invented to get rid of it.

"I'll get there as soon as I can. It's going to be a few more minutes before I can get away."

"Do you want my address?" I asked.

"Nope. I already have it—along with that for the rest of your gang members." I figured that I-told-you-so moment had arrived. Instead, he sighed. "Keep the doors locked, okay?"

"Will do. Charly's on her way over, so I won't be alone."

"Good. She'll know what to do if there's trouble before I get there."

"She will?" I asked. He must not have heard me because he ended the call without answering my question. I paced around the kitchen trying to decide what to do next. When the doorbell rang, I jumped about a foot off the ground. Domino woofed and dashed to the front door.

"Fix your hair," were the first words out of Charly's mouth once I let her inside. When I glanced at my image in the mirror near the front door, I could see why. My hair was standing up on end. "I'm going to put Emily and Domino outside, okay? Then you can show me what Domino found and did her best to bury."

While Charly let the dogs out, I slipped into the powder room and combed my hair. I leaned in to look at myself in the mirror and began an all too familiar slide into paranoia wondering why she'd mentioned my hair. Did it have to do with Hank's visit, or had she learned something more about my situation? I sighed and took a step backward away from the sink.

"Miriam Webster, you're becoming a kook!" I wagged my finger as I chided myself. "Keeping secrets isn't good for your mental health." All this sneaking around as a sleuth didn't help either. Especially with the prospect that a murderer on the loose had been on my front porch today. One with the audacity to shove something through the slot in my front door!

The image of Boo crossing the bridge that led to the beach from here gave me a shiver. Had he been here at my house? Dave Winick's drive by visit on the golf cart came to mind too. As I recalled the photos I'd found online, the smile he wore now seemed a tad crooked. From what Judi had told me, it just had to be Boo.

"I knew he'd been through the store because I'd catch a whiff of his cologne in the air."

When I returned to the kitchen, Charly had put on plastic gloves and was peering at that battered envelope. She gave it a sniff.

"Whew! That is strong, isn't it? Are you sure this is the same scent you noticed out on the bluff?"

"Yes. It's distinctive, don't you think? Besides, Domino's nose is better than mine, and I can't imagine another reason for her to react so strangely, can you? I'm sure you're correct that she's paired the scent with the incident out on Fitzgerald's Bluff."

"I'm dying to know what's in the envelope. We'll wait until Hank gets here and let him open it."

"I'm not as eager as you are to see what lovely message a strangler has left. Boo is my best guess at the identity of my visitor," I added. Before Charly could ask me who that was, I continued. "Let me make you a cup of tea and I'll tell you all I know about a man named Boo. Neely and I were going to do that this evening, but circumstances keep changing our plans today. I suppose she called you about having dinner here and our decision not to canvass the residents in the summer cottages."

"Yes, she did, but our conversation was brief. Neely said you have all sorts of information to share, including the lowdown on a boyfriend Diana called Boo, so I'd heard the odd name already."

"The two boys we met on the beach have a story about Howard Humphrey, too. I'm sure you'll find it interesting even though you already know he was renting the Sinclair Cottage. What clever brothers they are!"

"It's too bad they didn't go to the police right away." Charly shrugged. "Trust isn't easy when you're that young. I wish I could say knowing who you can confide in when you're in a pickle gets easier with age, but that's not necessarily true, is it?"

"No, it's not." I busied myself with the task of making our tea and changed the subject, once again, not wanting to get pulled into a deeper conversation about trust given what a fake I am. "Do you want Earl Grey or an herbal tea without the caffeine?"

"We've still got a long day ahead, so I'll take the caffeine. One of those scones Neely says we're having with dinner tonight, too, please."

"Consider it done!" I pulled out teacups and saucers and added two matching dessert plates. The lovely china set had been a wedding gift. It's one of the few treasured items I'd kept during my mad efforts to downsize when it became obvious I couldn't hang onto the house. I touched the lovely delicate pieces that always made me think about the fragile beauty of our lives.

"I wonder why so many people are bent on destroying themselves. Diana was beautiful. She obviously had men clamoring for her attention and must have had some talent as a singer since she had an agent and performed at clubs in and around San Francisco. One of the saleswomen we spoke to believed Diana was all about the thrill of the chase when it came to men—more a huntress than a siren as her coworker told the media. Ironic that she bore the name of the Roman goddess of the hunt." I shrugged, not sure why that seemed to matter.

"There are all sorts of theories about what leads someone like Diana into criminal activity. Thrill-seeking, yes, but there are others. Narcissism, lack of self-control, impulsivity, and a desire for wealth and success without being willing to put in the effort required to achieve those outcomes among them. After looking into her background, I can tell you that her troubles started in her teens. Her juvenile records were sealed, but have been reopened as part of the murder investigation. She was also picked up and questioned a couple of times about incidents that occurred in the clubs where she worked while she was still in the Bay Area. Life is tough enough without engaging in all the risky behavior she found so irresistible. It was all bound to catch up with her at some point." Charly sighed deeply before going on.

"People do change. Especially if someone can reach them when they're young. Past behavior is still the best predictor of future behavior. I didn't find any evidence in the record that she was abused or had an especially dysfunctional family life. As you said, though, she sure seemed bent on destroying herself. Why don't you give me the details about your discoveries today and connect the dots for me since Neely and I didn't have time to do that? I'd like to be sure I understand why you're so convinced Boo left the envelope that Domino found so disturbing."

"Sure, we should do that before Hank gets here." While I'd brought our tea to the table, Charly had let the two dogs back inside after their romp outdoors. They were napping side by side right now like a pair of perfect little angels. When Charly spoke Domino's name, they wagged their tails in tandem. At moments like this, it was hard to believe the chaos they could create when they gave into their wild side. "Let's hope Domino doesn't enjoy her new game so much she keeps on playing it—or that she doesn't teach it to Emily!"

"That's all I need! Emily's already quite capable of moving things from one part of the house to another and adept at hiding them from me. I live a life of mystery every day. Nothing like the kind of day you've had, though. Let's get through as much of it as we can before the law arrives."

For about twenty minutes, we drank our tea, ate our scones, and talked. Yes, I ate another one. There's comfort in both tea and sweets. I told Charly what Neely and I had learned about Diana, including the men in her life, her thieving, framing other people, and the reasons I figured that package had come from Boo.

Our conversation came to a sudden halt when both Domino and Emily began barking. The two dogs settled down as the four of us went in pack formation to answer the door. Hank stood on my porch gazing at the view of the blue Pacific Ocean that I couldn't help noticing was almost the same color as his eyes. Much to my surprise, he wasn't alone.

"Come on in, Detective."

"They don't call it Seaview Cottages for nothing, do they, Hemingway?" He laughed as he said that. He must have noticed the plaque hanging on the gate that designated my place as the Hemingway Cottage. Of course, he'd heard Joe Torrance call me that at the Blue Haven Pro Shop today, too. I tried to accept his comments as friendly, almost collegial, inspired by the intoxicating vision of the ocean.

"No, they don't," I replied.

"This is Karen Vaughan," he added. The young woman with him displayed a no-nonsense demeanor as she stepped inside my home and gave my hand a single shake. "Karen's with the crime lab. She's going to take custody of the evidence and carry it directly to the lab, right?"

"Yes, Sir," she responded. "What have we got?"

"Follow me." When we arrived in the kitchen, the

crime scene investigator set a case she'd brought with her on the table next to the laundry basket. She put on a pair of gloves, spread a sheet of plastic on my table, and opened a clear plastic bag. Then she picked up the envelope by a corner, slit it open with a little retractable blade that must have come from that kit. In another moment, she slid the contents from the envelope revealing sheets of paper that she spread out on the plastic. I breathed a sigh of relief that no handwritten death threat glared at us. Nor was there one of those cut and paste jobs made of words or letters from magazines like I'd seen in an episode of *Columbo* or *Murder She Wrote*.

"May I take a look?" Charly asked. She didn't wait for a reply before pulling a clean pair of gloves from a box in the woman's crime lab kit. Karen Vaughan moved out of the way as Charly examined each piece of paper.

"Well, well, well," she said as she reviewed the items. "Diana Durand did have a knack for getting herself into trouble. Others, too! These papers must contain the information she was trying to sell to Edgar. It's too bad he didn't buy it from her since he might have found it very interesting."

When Charly got to the last sheet of paper, there was a note penned on it in big bold print.

Diana didn't deserve to die.

"What does it all mean?" I asked. Charly proceeded to give us the details of a plot to gain control of the Seaview Cottages community by convincing members of the HOA to change management companies. In effect, giving control to a shell company owned by the Blue Haven Resort Properties Development Group run by Dave Winick. The documents included several memos and emails that Diana must have printed out from Dave Winick's computer or copied from his files. One of the memos had handwritten notes in the margins that he must have made. In them, two HOA board members were mentioned by name—Greta Bishop and Peggy Clayton.

"There's no evidence here that they've done anything yet to undermine or discredit the current management company at Seaview Cottages. It does say 'on our team' next to their names," Charly noted.

"I know shell companies are used to cover up dirty tricks and illegal activity, but why would they need to do that?"

"Dave Winick's memo describes plans to transform Seaview Cottages into The Blue Haven Resort Residences by putting it into the hands of 'new management.' On the face of it, it sounds legit—especially if he argued that new management would be better management than what we've got already. We've talked about the fact a deal might be in the works, Miriam, and even considered it might be on the up and up. With a little strategic *mis*management, our community that's struggling to stay afloat could sink like a stone. A shell company would be a perfect way to hide the parties behind the dirty-dealing."

I nodded. It had been so much easier for Pete and our accountant to keep me in the dark. No shell company needed—just a gullible woman who didn't question her husband's repeated delays in reviewing financial plans for a retirement that never happened anyway. Was that why I'm now so intent on getting to the bottom of the latest mystery?

"Devers has mumbled about Seaview Cottages going under, but I figured he was being a crank," Hank said.

"As far as I can tell from reviewing the books, it's not that dire, Detective. There's a plan in place to retrofit and repair the infrastructure while keeping the reserves at the level required by law. As residents, we're all being asked to chip in more to make that happen. I'm not sure what Charly means, specifically, by strategic mismanagement, but we are vulnerable. Charly probably has a better idea of what it would take to push us into bankruptcy or legal trouble."

"Yes, I do! All sorts of hanky-panky involving the mishandling of funds could make our community's money problems worse. Violating the rules and regulations that govern fifty-five plus communities could get us in more trouble, too. Rules violations carry fines or can trigger court intervention. Legal fees piled on top of fines could push us toward insolvency. Maybe that's what Dave Winick intended to do. If I were Greta Bishop or Peggy Clayton, I would have gone to the police when Diana was killed and told them everything I'd learned as a member of Winick's team. But what do I know?"

"Plenty!" I replied spontaneously. "Even if our illustrious board members haven't reached that conclusion, Boo has. Dropping off these pages would explain what he was doing around here earlier today."

"You should examine the documents for yourself, Hank. While you're at it, take a sniff of the envelope." As she said that, Karen Vaughan didn't wait for the detective to act. She picked up that envelope with a gloved hand, waved it under her nose, and withdrew it quickly. Then she waved it under his.

"It's a strong cologne, Sir." I launched into my explanation about why I figured Boo was the one who used the cologne on the package. Hank didn't say anything at first, as a sad, weary expression settled onto his face.

"Unfortunately, we'll never know. When I told you to keep your doors locked, it's because there's been another death. The name we have for him isn't Boo, it's Bradley Richards, and he's well-known to my colleagues in the police force in San Francisco. Apparently, he was an illegal street fighter who ended up as a bouncer when he couldn't take any more punches to his liver and kidneys. By then, his brains weren't in very good shape either, which probably explains how he fell under Diana Durand's spell. The San Francisco police went straight to his apartment when I called to report that he'd been murdered. They found stacks of merchandise from Blue Haven Resort shops. Apparently, he wasn't very skilled at fencing the goods Diana funneled to him."

"Alf and Alyssa Gardener must have had it right after all when they said Diana was demanding money from him!" Charly exclaimed.

"Given she also slapped him, she'd be a likely suspect in his murder if she was still with us. Do you have any idea who killed him since she's already dead?"

"That's a good question. He wasn't strangled, so it's not immediately apparent the same person killed both Diana Durand and Bradley Richards. He was hit on the head and then either fell or was shoved into the water. His body was found floating in a tide pool near Dickens' Dune." I gasped.

"That's where you thought he might be headed, Hank!"

"Yes, it's too bad we didn't catch up with him sooner. He never showed up at the parking lot where we had an officer waiting to pick him up."

"Oh, good grief, another murder on the beach near Seaview Cottages," Charly muttered. "We won't need to worry about Winick's scam if this trouble doesn't stop soon. Who's going to use the golf course, the restaurant, or buy a cottage in the murder capital of the California Central Coast?"

"This isn't two crimes, but one crime with two parts," I offered in a feeble effort to console Charly. "Once Hank gets to the bottom of it, all the bad press will clear up."

"It's time for another chat with Dave Winick. We're also still trying to catch up with Howard Humphrey, who hasn't returned to the golf shop or Sinclair Cottage. He has some explaining to do, too, and not just about the fact he was with Diana shortly before someone killed her. When I asked the San Francisco police what they'd found in Bradley Richards' apartment, top of the line golf clubs came up right away."

"Are you saying he was stealing from the resort, too?" I asked.

"Either that, or looking the other way while Diana helped herself to the merchandise in his shop." I nodded.

"He wouldn't have been the first one to do that. Mark Hudson must have told you about the trouble Mike Evans got into when Diana ripped off guests while he was escorting them to their rooms."

"Yes. I'm giving Howard Humphrey the benefit of the

doubt by suggesting Diana used him in the same way," Hank said.

"Well, he must not have figured it out if they were planning to fly away together. Maybe Mike Evans caught up with her," Charley suggested.

"Mike Evans' alibi is airtight. If Howard did figure out what she'd done, he might have decided she wasn't going to get a third chance to betray him. The trip could have been a ruse to lure her out to the dunes and kill her." Hank shook his head. "At least we can place him with her at the scene that morning, so he's got some tough questions to answer if we can ever get our hands on him. I can't believe I let him get away." A rush of guilt came over me when his eyes settled on me. I stammered a little when I spoke.

"Hey...uh, I'm sorry if our timing wasn't so great when Neely and I showed up. I'm sorry there's been another murder, too. I get it if Howard killed Diana, but why kill Boo?"

"I agree. It's more likely someone discovered Boo intended to pass along the information he dropped off here today," Charly suggested.

"And tried to stop him before he could do it, right?" I asked.

"Precisely!" she responded. "If we're lucky, Winick or whoever killed Boo believes he succeeded and the killing's over."

"Don't count on it!" Hand exclaimed. "Luck won't be enough to keep you all out of trouble if you're wrong," Hank warned. "It's no accident Bradley Richards picked you as the person to receive his message, Miriam, given the stir you've caused the past couple of days. I've told you to stop snooping already, but I'm going to say it again! No more visits to the places where our victims or suspects liked to hang out. No more questions, in disguise or otherwise. No more background checks either, by the way."

Hank fixed Charly with a withering gaze when he said that. She didn't flinch, but reluctantly agreed with a nod. Then Hank softened his voice as his eyes dropped to the pages spread out on my kitchen table.

"I don't mean to be ungrateful. Your efforts have been remarkably helpful. Let's call it 'beginner's luck' if you believe in that sort of thing. What good will it do for you to save the Seaview Cottages community from going into default if you all aren't around to enjoy the view?"

"I appreciate your concern. I'd be happy not to have more clues end up on my doorstep," I grumbled.

"The best way to do that is to lie low. No more scone bribes. It's not just Mark Hudson who gave you away, either. Deputy Devers tells me the news traveled fast at the resort about a Hollywood scriptwriter buying information about Diana Durand with scones." Then Hank broke into a smile. "Okay, so maybe one more little bribe won't hurt. How about a couple of those scones to keep us from turning you in for 'promoting interference with the course of justice?'" My mouth fell open as he threw the words I'd spoken earlier back at me. "You won't blab will you, Karen?"

"No, Sir." She responded. "Blab about what, Sir?" She asked. I don't believe the woman asked that question as a joke. She appeared to be genuinely puzzled as she assembled the pages for transport back to the lab.

"You're a good sport, Karen. Your boss is a big kidder, isn't he?" I asked.

"If you say so." She stared at me as if she was still processing the preceding social interaction. Then it must have all come together for her because she smiled so broadly that a dimple appeared in her cheek. "Do we really get scones?"

"Yes, you do!" I packed two little boxes of scones while Karen put her kit back together and closed it up. "Here you go. I'm counting on you to destroy the evidence as soon as possible."

Hank didn't hesitate. He had one of those scones in hand as he headed to the front door. After a slight delay, Karen got it too. When she left my front porch, she turned to show me the hand that had held a scone was now empty.

"Scone? What scone?" She asked in a muffled voice, still chewing the last bite. I gave her a thumbs up which she returned.

"Hank, please give me a call when you've picked up Humphrey and Winick, okay?" Charly asked as Hank stepped out onto the porch. He turned around and replied to Charly, but his clear blue eyes were on me.

"Sure, but it's going to cost you. Can you bake cookies, Miriam?"

"Of course—any kind in particular?" I asked. My skin prickled at the prospect of seeing the detective again when he collected his payment. A kaleidoscope of emotions rushed through me too. Anticipation, apprehension, bewilderment, and pleasure all competed to hold sway over me.

"Surprise me! You're good at that." Happiness won out when a broad smile spread over his face before he dashed away.

When I turned around, Charly was grinning. I was, too. My initial impulse was to squelch the good feelings, or at least mask them. Somehow, I didn't believe I could hide much from Charly, so I didn't try. Besides, it had been a long time since I'd been this happy.

"He has no idea how good you are at surprises, does he?" Charly chuckled. Her eyes twinkled. "Emily! Time to go home. We'll be back to visit Domino later tonight." The petite woman bent down and swept Emily up into her arms.

I mumbled—not in reply to her question, but barely coherent babbling about seeing her later. I'd just stepped away when the doorbell rang again. Domino and I dashed back to the door. When I opened it, Charly was standing on the porch holding Emily.

"Did you forget something?" That's when several things happened at once. A breeze blew in off the ocean and carried with it a whiff of that cologne. Domino must have noticed it too, because she pushed past me, stood up, putting her front paws on the door, and tried to shut it. A foot wedged in the opening prevented it from closing.

19

Good as Gold

"THAT'S RUDE, MIRIAM, or should I say Tara? We're here for some of those scones we've heard so much about. They're all the buzz around Big Blue, aren't they Howard?" Dave Winick gave Charly and Howard Humphrey a shove. They all stepped inside, and Dave Winick shut the door behind him. That's when I saw the gun. Domino growled.

I couldn't tell which man was wearing the cologne, but I sure could smell it. Domino did too, and she didn't like it. She backed up, arched her back, and barked loudly. That set Emily off so that both dogs were barking. As Emily grew more agitated, she squirmed and worked her way out of Charly's arms and onto the floor in my foyer. She began to circle us frantically, her leash trailing after her.

"Shut that dog up, or I will!" Dave Winick pointed the gun at Emily who ran behind Domino for protection.

"You fire that gun and half the neighborhood is going to be on the phone to the police," Charly said.

"What is it you really want?" I asked emboldened by Charly's challenge. I mimicked the firm, calm voice she'd used. The sound of our voices settled the dogs down. They were both still on high alert, but had quit barking and stood motionless. My mind reeled as I tried to make sense of the strange tableau in my foyer. Among the motionless figures, a dejected looking Howard Humphrey stood there with his shoulders slumped and his eyes lowered.

"I want those papers Bradley Richards gave you." My heart jumped into my throat. I glanced at Charly who shook her head no which I took to mean that I shouldn't tell him the truth that those papers were long gone.

"What makes you believe I have them?" I asked.

"Tell her, Howie."

"Boo—Bradley told me you were asking questions about Diana's death and when he found out you live here at Seaview Cottages, he figured you'd do something about it if you knew what was really going on. He didn't trust the cops to care one way or the other about finding out what happened to Diana. I..." Winick poked Howard with his gun.

"That's enough. I'll take those papers now. Then we'll be on our way. I've wiped the computer and shredded the originals in my office after Diana got herself killed. Those copies are the only proof that anything was ever in the works to speed things along and bring this pathetic place to its inevitable end. I should have known better than to let Diana stay at my condo when Edgar cut her off." He shook his head.

"Is that why you killed her?" I asked. Dave Winick's head shot up.

"I didn't do it. Howie, here, says he didn't do it either."

"You're not saying it was Boo, are you?" Charly asked. "I don't believe that for a minute. Why would he leave those papers for Miriam and encourage her to snoop into Diana's murder if it led back to him?"

"Who knows or cares? She had it coming after all the double-crosses she pulled. Maybe Boo was trying to mislead you by throwing me under the bus. He wouldn't have had any trouble wringing her neck that's for sure."

"Stop it, Dave. Boo loved her just like I did, and he had nothing to do with double-crossing or misleading anyone. You know that." Howard stared directly at Dave, and then looked at me.

"I had breakfast with Diana that morning after a night out celebrating. She'd found a buyer for the information she stole from Dave. We were going to use the money to get away for a fresh start. I have a small trust fund from Uncle Edgar that kicks in on my birthday in a few weeks. I tried to convince her we could get by on it, but she wanted to leave sooner and with a bundle of cash, so she pushed to make one last deal." A hitch in his voice stopped Howard. He took a couple of deep breaths before speaking again.

"I left Diana alone on the beach, so it's my fault she was killed. I was only gone a little while to get a decent signal on my cell phone. When I got back, she was dead. I panicked because she'd been killed so close to the place I'm renting. That's when I got the idea to call Boo to help me put her into the water. I hoped it would look as if she'd drowned. When Boo and I got back to Fitzgerald's Bluff, you, your dog, and all your friends had shown up. You'd seen her like that, but I thought no one would believe you if the body was gone."

"If you'd cleaned up the site and gotten rid of her belongings you might have had a better chance of pulling that off," Charly said.

"We planned to do that, but you all came back again with the deputy and your dogs, so we had to leave. I don't know who killed her. Boo thought Dave did it and didn't want him to get away with it. That's why he was going to give you a copy of the papers Diana took."

"You're wearing that cologne today—were you hiding out there on the bluff that morning?" I asked.

"Boo and I were hiding, but he's the one who had it on then. Diana loved it because it's from Paris. I don't wear it much since it bothers Uncle Edgar. I put it on today because it reminds me of her." As Howard spoke, a big fat tear slid down his flushed face.

"Oh, please. She was a pain in the…" Dave didn't get to finish his sentence.

"Don't say that!" Howard suddenly flew at Winick. That earned him a crack on the head from the butt of Dave Winick's gun. Howard crumpled to the ground as Domino lunged at Dave, too.

In another instant, Emily circled Dave, yapping loudly. Her leash coiled around his ankles, loosely. Then Charly sprang into action, grabbed the end of Emily's leash and gave it a yank. Using her front paws, Domino caught Dave on his chest as he struggled to remain standing, shoved him off balance, and he tumbled to the floor.

The gun flew, and I grabbed it. When I turned around, Charly had Dave Winick pinned to the ground with a bony knee in his stomach.

"Don't move," I said. He quit struggling when he saw me pointing the gun at him. I wasn't sure I could pull the trigger, but I did my best to look mean and sound nasty.

"Call Hank and let's get this wrapped up," Charly said in a matter of fact tone.

"I don't believe I need to do that. Listen!" Right before the situation went ballistic, I'd heard a siren, and it was much louder now. When I backed up a step and looked out the window, I saw Deputy Devers pull up across the street in his SUV. Hank Miller pulled up right behind him. Both men ran from their cars. By the time they got to my porch, I had the front door open.

"Come in. You're right on time for Charly's demonstration of Brazilian jiu-jitsu," I quipped as the two police officers took in the scene. I handed the gun to Hank. "This belongs to Dave." As Charly stood up, Devers pulled out his handcuffs. He put them on Dave and then pulled him to his feet.

"Lawyer. I want my lawyer," Dave Winick bellowed.

"What about Howard?" Devers asked, ignoring Dave's demand.

"Howard was just about to tell us who killed Diana Durand and Bradley Richards," Charly said.

"I was?" Howard asked as he struggled to sit up, holding his head. I could hardly believe he was conscious after that blow. There wasn't any blood, so maybe he hadn't been hit as hard as I feared when he'd slumped to the floor in my foyer.

"Who was going to buy that information from Diana?" I asked.

"This crazy coworker who'd been stalking Diana. The

one Diana set up and Dave hung out to dry when Diana was about to get busted by security for stealing from the Blue Moon Boutique. Judi Stephenson was angry with Diana, but she said she wanted to get back at Dave and Blue Haven Resort more. She kept after Diana—asking for proof about the favors he'd done for her—including telling her about the security team that was on its way so Diana could plant merchandise in Judi's drawer."

"Shut up you idiot! Lawyer!" Dave shouted.

"No. You shut up!" Howard replied in an emphatic tone. "Diana did better than that. She promised Judi information about a big scam Dave was running."

"We know about that," Charly responded. Dave's head spun around almost like Linda Blair in that scene from the *Exorcist*.

"Lawyer," he said once again. This time it sounded more like a plea than a command.

"So, what happened?" Charly asked.

"We took the money from Judi when she met us in the parking lot of the truck stop. Boo told me later that Diana had found another buyer willing to pay more, so she'd stiffed Judi. She took the money and gave her some worthless memos from Dave's computer."

"How much?" I asked, interrupting him. "How much money did Judi Stephenson pay for the information?"

"Twenty-five thousand dollars."

"I can't imagine where she got that kind of money." I couldn't come up with that kind of money unless a bank would give me an equity loan on my cottage. I had a more pressing question, though. "So, who killed Diana?"

"I never saw Judi after we left her in the parking lot.

She must have followed us back to the beach area. When I found Diana, she'd been strangled with a scarf like the ones she'd planted in Judi's drawer. Diana's purse had been dumped and the money Judi had given her was gone." He shrugged. "Things don't always work out as you plan, do they?"

"No, they don't," Charly said. "Not for you and Diana, and not for Judi Stephenson. It'll be easy enough to figure out if she borrowed that kind of money recently. She must have had to make several withdrawals to get that much cash without raising suspicions at a bank. I can check. I'll bet if Midge asks her friend, Doward, he can place Judi at the truck stop that morning."

"No!" Hank said. "No checking on her bank accounts, Charly. Midge isn't going to ask her friend, Doward, or anyone else about Judi Stephenson. What does it take to get you all to back off?"

"I told you the members of this gang of old ladies don't listen to reason. You want me to round them up and take them in for obstruction of justice?"

"Will you stop it, Darnell? What you can do is take Winick and Humphrey to the station. I'll be there later, and we can sort out what charges to bring against them."

"What about Boo?" I asked. "Who killed him?"

"Dave did it," Howard said sadly. Dave was about to object, but Howard cut him off.

"You can holler lawyer all you want, but I saw you do it." Howard paused to look the man in the eye before he began speaking, once again, to the rest of us.

"Dave wanted those papers back. When Boo said he'd given them to you, Miriam, Dave hit him over the head with the butt of his gun even harder than he just hit me." Howard stared defiantly at Winick who glared at him from a few feet away. Then Howard's shoulders slumped again. "I'm not sure Dave was trying to kill him, but Boo fell into the water. I begged Dave to let me try to help Boo, but getting the papers mattered more to him."

"Why am I not surprised?" Charly huffed.

"He let me call 911, but I knew help would get there too late. Dave searched Boo's car that he'd in the lot nearby, hoping he'd lied about giving them to you. When we got here, Dave thought he'd have a better chance of getting you to cooperate if he brought your friend in here at gunpoint. I tried to tell him to forget it. I knew if Boo had given you those papers you would have turned them over to the police right away. Dave didn't believe me. He was convinced you'd use them to blackmail him."

"He was wrong and landed in a trap of his own making, just like Diana," Charly said shaking her head.

"Let's go," Devers said, speaking directly to Howard. "Do I need to cuff you?"

"No. I'm tired of running. Besides, even if I ran, Diana wouldn't be there anyway. She was the best and the worst thing that ever happened to me. I have the scarf Judi used to kill her, Detective. If you want it, I'll tell you where it's hidden."

"Tell Darnell and he'll send someone from the crime lab to get it, okay?" As Darnell left my house with the two men in tow, Hank added. "I'm going to pick up Judi Stephenson myself. I'll also send someone to have another chat with Midge's friend, Doward. I'm sure you're right that he didn't miss a thing that morning and can identify

Judi Stephenson as someone he saw with Diana and Howard that morning."

"Take it easy on her, will you?" I asked. "I'm not sure why I'm asking you that since I'm sure Howard's right that she murdered Diana Durand. I don't believe she intended it to work out that way. Being swindled by Diana a second time must have sent her over the edge."

"I hear you. We all have our breaking point, don't we?" Hank asked as he walked out my door.

"True. But not us—not today anyway." Charly was picking up items that had been tossed around in the melee. "Let's get these dogs a reward for their help bringing down a villain."

"At least, given Howard's statement, there was only one murder near Seaview Cottages," Midge said several hours later when we'd gone through the entire ordeal for everyone after dinner.

"Manslaughter's not much better," Marty added.

"Don't worry. It'll all come out that most of this mess is centered at the hoity-t0ity resort and not here. Not just murder, but conspiracy, theft, blackmail, coworkers framing each other, and a member of management fooling around with his employee—what a disaster!" Neely's wild curls flew as she made that statement.

"I'm sure their PR folks are working to manage the trouble in their little piece of paradise. Dave Winick's already been put on leave without pay pending the outcome of the legal actions he's facing—manslaughter's a career killer even if he can wriggle out of the consequences for his other misdeeds," Charly observed.

"Howard's going to pay since he played a part in Diana's theft ring. What a waste of his life," I said. "This has to be hard on Edgar even though he'll do what he can to help Howard."

"At least Howard's got someone to help him. Judi Stephenson's pretty much on her own," Charly added. Somehow, Charly had found the energy after that showdown at my house to hound her police department contacts, so she could come to dinner with the latest updates. That wasn't all she'd done since she left my house.

"Thankfully, we have two fewer troublesome HOA Board members to complain about now that Greta Bishop and Peggy Clayton have resigned. Good work bringing them to their senses, Charly," Marty added. Charly took a little bow.

"My pleasure, I assure you."

"Maybe we can get more done around here like that rule change to let us be more flexible about the age restriction issue. I couldn't understand why Greta Bishop was opposed to it given that it ought to bolster resales. What a rat! More vigorous resales weren't in the interest of Mr. Winick's master plan to sink us, though, were they?" Neely pinched her nose closed and made glug-glug sounds as if she were under water.

"Let's hope her Garbo Cottage will be up for sale soon. I can't believe she'll stay in the community once people realize she tried to sell us out. Can you believe she and Peggy fell for that con artist?" Midge groused.

"Charming psychopaths with pretty faces can be awfully persuasive," Charly asserted. "At least when we get that rule change through we can get Miriam off the hook.

When were you planning to tell us what happened to Pete? His obit in the Columbus Dispatch is sketchy." I squirmed. All eyes were on me.

"You all know about this?" I asked.

"We suspected something was up. Charly's the one who figured it out," Neely replied. "Let's fix it, okay? We need you as one of our Grand Old Lady Detectives. That's obvious." Charly grinned at me.

"She can help us keep that fine-looking detective happy," Neely added, giggling.

"Yeah, it's all about the scones, isn't it?" Midge chimed in, smirking.

"Cookies, too, don't forget!" Marty added. I felt such a mix of emotions—relief, shame, gratitude, and fear about what was going to happen next. I could barely breathe.

"My head is spinning. Give me a break, okay? I'm sorry I wasn't more straightforward about all of this. The last year has been a huge mess. I... I..." I would have had more to say, but the doorbell rang.

"Who could that be at this hour?" Marty asked.

"It's not even nine o'clock, for goodness' sake. Maybe it's Carl and Joe trying to get the scoop from the Grand Old Lady Detectives—who've got it going on!" Neely said and did one of those little head shifts that go with some hip Hollywood dance.

The doorbell rang again. Domino and Emily were on their feet after the first ring. Now they both barked and dashed to the door. I ran after them with the others on my heels. I peeked through the peephole in the door and then opened it wide.

"Hello, ladies," Joe said. "Uh, sorry. Hello, women!"

"We brought you a paying customer now that you've gone into business for yourselves," Carl added pointing to Robyn Chappell who stood between Carl and Joe.

"Who told you that?" I asked. Their eyes were on Charly in a flash!

"Didn't you believe us when we said we're Charly's angels?" Carl replied.

"Robyn needs to talk to you. Good as Gold ought to be their motto, Robyn. If they can't help you, nobody can." Joe waved an arm as she stepped into my foyer. She didn't wait another minute to get to the point.

"Someone's been in my cottage," she said. "More than once."

"She's not talking about the sitting in my chair, eating my porridge kind of visitor either," Carl added. "And it's not the landlord. We checked."

"Who do you think it is?" I asked. "Why don't you call the police?"

As I asked that question, Hank's smiling face whisked through my mind. It wasn't too surprising that when I said police his image was the one I conjured up. Hank was a far more appealing option than Deputy Devers was, and not strictly because of his skills as a lawman. I'd caught myself thinking of the detective several times since he'd left. Robyn's next statement confirmed that, no matter what the reason, I was right to prefer Hank to Darnell.

"I have," Robyn replied. "Deputy Devers called me a crazy lady—one among many at Seaview Cottages!"

"Why?" I asked.

"Because it's Shakespeare's ghost and he's looking for

something in my cottage! Maybe I am crazy. I don't want to move out of Shakespeare's Cottage. I love it—and this entire place, too."

"Don't sweat it, Robyn. They know all about the daffy old dame treatment from Devers. They won't let it happen to you." Carl nodded in enthusiastic agreement with Joe's statement.

I sighed heavily. Carl and Joe were right, of course. How could we let that happen? I wasn't convinced Robyn was being troubled by a ghost, but something was going on. She was clearly distraught. How could we turn our backs on her?

"Do you like scones?" I asked, motioning for our visitors to follow as we all paraded back into the kitchen.

"What makes you believe it's Shakespeare's ghost?" Neely asked.

"That's a good question," Marty added. "It could be any dead person, couldn't it?'

What a day! What a year! I thought. What on earth can happen next?

—THE END—

Thanks so much for reading *A Body on Fitzgerald's Bluff*, the first book in my Seaview Cottages Cozy Mystery series. I hope if you enjoyed meeting Miriam Webster, Domino, and the other residents of the Seaview Cottages Community you'll leave me a review on Amazon, Goodreads, and Bookbub.

I'd love to hear from you if you have feedback for me or questions about this or any other book I've written. Feel free to contact me by email at burke.59@osu.edu.

Book 2 in the Seaview Cottages Cozy Mystery series, *The Murder of Shakespeare's Ghost,* will be out soon. To keep up with news about the release of that book, with sales and giveaways, I'd love for you to subscribe to my newsletter: desertcitiesmystery.com.

While you're waiting for the next installment of murder and mayhem with the Grand Old Lady Detectives, why not check out the books in one of the other series I write? You can find them all on my Amazon author page amazon.com/Anna-Celeste-Burke/e/B00H8J4IQS.

RECIPES

MUFFINS
12 full-size or 24 mini muffins

Ingredients
2 cups pastry flour or Unbleached All-Purpose Flour*
1/2 cup sugar
1/2 teaspoon salt
1 tablespoon baking powder
1 cup milk
1/4 cup vegetable oil or melted butter
2 large eggs
1 teaspoon vanilla extract
white sugar, for topping

Directions
Preheat your oven to 425°F. Lightly grease the cups of a standard 12-cup muffin pan. Or line the cups with papers and grease the papers.

Mix the dry ingredients.

Blend the liquid ingredients—milk, oil or butter, eggs, and vanilla.

Pour the wet ingredients into the dry ingredients. Whisk together just until it's all blended—about 20 seconds should do it. Don't overmix—it's fine to have some lumps so don't keep stirring!

Fill the cups of the muffin pan two-thirds to three-quarters full. Sprinkle with sparkling white sugar, if desired.

Bake the muffins for 15 to 20 minutes, or until a toothpick inserted into the middle of one of the center muffins comes out clean. Remove them from the oven, and as soon as you can handle them turn them out of the pan onto a rack to cool.

For berry or fruit muffins: Add 1 1/2 cups of berries to the recipe (or finely chopped, well-drained fresh fruit: peaches, apples, etc.; or chopped dried fruit). To make sure berries or fruit stay evenly distributed throughout the batter, add to the dry ingredients and mix until coated before adding the liquid ingredients. This prevents them from sinking once the liquids are blended in.

For oatmeal muffins: Instead of using 2 cups of flour, use 1 cup rolled oats and 1 1/4 cups flour. You can also substitute brown sugar for granulated. These muffins don't rise as high as the basic muffins, but they certainly taste wonderful!

*If you can't tolerate gluten, use your favorite gluten free flour instead

QUEEN CITY CHILI
Serves 6-8

Ingredients

1 large onion, chopped*
1 pound extra-lean ground beef (hamburger)
1 clove garlic, minced
1 tablespoon chile powder
1 teaspoon ground allspice
1 teaspoon ground cinnamon
1 teaspoon ground cumin*
1 teaspoon ground ginger*
1/2 teaspoon red (cayenne) pepper
1/2 teaspoon salt
1 1/2 tablespoons unsweetened cocoa or 1/2 ounce grated
    unsweetened chocolate*
1 (15-ounce) can tomato sauce
1 tablespoon Worcestershire sauce
1 tablespoon cider vinegar
1/2 cup water
1 (16-ounce) package uncooked dried spaghetti pasta
Oyster crackers

*These are all optional since some fans of this chili will tell you these items weren't in the original recipe—basically this is a ground beef chili accented with a blend of Middle Eastern spices. Experiment until you find the blend that's perfect for you!

Toppings

Shredded Cheddar Cheese
Chopped Onion
Kidney Beans [canned, heated in a little of the chili]

Directions

In a large frying pan over medium-high heat, sauté onion, ground beef, garlic, and chili powder until ground beef is slightly cooked. Ground beef should be stirred so it's fine, not clumpy or chunky [some cooks say put the beef through a food processor before cooking].

Add allspice, cinnamon, cumin, ginger, cayenne pepper, salt, unsweetened cocoa or chocolate, tomato sauce, Worcestershire sauce, cider vinegar, and water. Reduce heat to low and simmer, uncovered, 1 hour 30 minutes. Remove from heat. [Some say it's even better if you make this a day ahead and reheat!]

Cook spaghetti according to package directions and transfer onto individual serving plates.

Ladle Cincinnati Chili mixture over the cooked spaghetti and serve with toppings of your choice.

Have it your way

Two-way chili: served on spaghetti
Three-way chili: add mounds of finely shredded cheddar cheese
Four-way chili: add chopped onions on top of the cheese
Five-way chili: add a ladle or two of kidney beans on top of all the rest!
Serve with oyster crackers on the side!

DEATH BY CHOCOLATE CAKE
Makes 12 Slices

Ingredients

<u>Cake</u>
4 cups all-purpose flour
2 cups sugar
1 cup brown sugar
2 1/4 cups cocoa powder
3 teaspoons baking soda
3 teaspoons baking powder
1 pinch of kosher salt
1 1/2 cups melted butter
6 large eggs, lightly beaten
2 1/2 cups espresso or strong black coffee
2 1/2 cups buttermilk
1 tablespoon pure vanilla extract

<u>Ganache Filling</u>
1 cup heavy cream
2 tablespoons butter
2 cups chocolate chips milk, semi-sweet, or dark
2 tablespoons brewed coffee or espresso
1 pinch of kosher salt

<u>Frosting</u>
3 cups butter—softened
7 1/2 cups powdered sugar
2 1/4 cups cocoa powder
1 tablespoon pure vanilla extract
1 pinch of kosher salt

3/4 c. heavy cream (plus more if necessary)
4 cups semisweet chocolate chips—divided

Directions

<u>Cake</u>
Preheat oven to 350°. Line three 8" round cake pans with parchment and spray with nonstick cooking spray.

In a large bowl, whisk together flour, sugars, cocoa powder, baking soda, baking powder and salt. Add the melted butter, eggs, coffee, buttermilk and vanilla and whisk until smooth.

Divide batter evenly among the cake pans. Bake until a toothpick inserted into the center comes out clean, about 35 minutes. Let cool completely on wire racks before removing from pans.

<u>Filling</u>
Add heavy cream and butter to a small saucepan and heat on low heat until the butter has melted, and the cream is warmed throughout.

Add chocolate chips to a large glass or nonreactive bowl. Pour the warmed cream and butter mixture over the chocolate chips. Add in the brewed coffee and a pinch of salt. Allow to stand for about 3-5 minutes to soften the chocolate chips completely.

Stir briskly to combine and until smooth. Allow to cool then spread between layers of cake and assemble.

Frosting

In a large bowl using a hand mixer, beat together butter, powdered sugar, cocoa powder, vanilla, and salt. Blend in the heavy cream (adding more by the tablespoon until consistency is creamy but can hold peaks).

Cover the entire cake with frosting. Then use your hands to cover the cake chocolate chips—about 3 cups. In the microwave, melt one cup of chocolate chips—start with 1 minute on a medium setting. If necessary, continue to heat in 15 second intervals. Drizzle melted chocolate over cake and serve.

VANILLA BEAN SCONES
8 scones

Ingredients

Scones
2 cups all-purpose flour
1 tablespoon baking powder
3/4 teaspoon salt
1/3 cup granulated vanilla bean sugar [see note below
    about this sugar]
1/2 cup cold, unsalted butter cut into 1/2-inch cubes
1/2 cup heavy cream or half and half—cold
1/2 teaspoon vanilla extract
1 large egg—cold

Glaze
1 1/2 cups powdered sugar
Caviar from inside 1 vanilla bean (or substitute 1 teaspoon
    of vanilla bean paste)
2-3 tablespoons cream or half and half as need for desired
    consistency

Directions
Preheat the oven to 400 degrees F. Line a baking sheet
with parchment paper or silicone baking mats and set
aside.

Combine the flour, baking powder, salt, and vanilla sugar
together in a large bowl. Work the cold butter into the
flour mixture with a pastry cutter, fork or with your clean
fingertips until you have a coarse mixture with pea sized
pieces of butter. Make a well in the center of the flour
mixture.

Whisk the eggs with the milk and vanilla extract until blended. Gradually pour the milk mixture into the flour mixture, stirring until just combined. Do not overmix.

Transfer the dough to a clean, lightly floured surface. With a lightly floured hand knead the dough by folding it in thirds toward the center and then flatten—repeat 3 times. Pat the dough out to an 8 or 9-inch circle (about 3/4-inch-thick) and cut into 8 triangle shaped pieces.

Use a spatula to arrange the scones about 1/2-inch apart on the prepared baking sheet. Bake the scones in the preheated oven for about 15-18 minutes, until golden brown around the edges. Allow scones to cool for 2 minutes on the baking sheet before transferring them to a wire rack to cool.

While the scones are cooling, prepare the glaze. Place the powdered sugar into a small bowl. Stir the vanilla bean caviar into the cream or half and half. Slowly whisk the into the powdered sugar until smooth. Glaze should be fluid yet spoon-able. Add additional milk or powdered sugar as needed to reach the desired consistency.

Once the scones have cooled, spoon the glaze over each scone covering it completely—you can spread the glaze with the back of the spoon. Allow the scones to rest until the glaze sets before serving.

Leftover scones may be stored at room temperature, lightly tented with aluminum foil for a day or in an airtight container for a couple of days.

VANILLA BEAN SUGAR

Ingredients
1 whole vanilla bean
2 cups sugar

Directions
Place the sugar into an airtight container like a mason jar.

Slice the vanilla bean open lengthwise. With the back of knife, scrape the seeds into the container and mix with the sugar. Bury the bean pod in the sugar, too, and seal tightly with lid. Store until ready to use. Use as you would regular granulated sugar.

SHOO FLY PIE
Serves 6-8

Ingredients
1/2 cup molasses
1 teaspoon baking soda
1 cup boiling water
1 pinch salt
1 1/2 cups all-purpose flour
1 cup brown sugar
3/4 cup butter
1/2 teaspoon ground cinnamon
1 (9 inch) unbaked pie crust

Directions
Preheat oven to 375 degrees F (190 degrees C).

In a medium bowl, dissolve the soda in the molasses and stir until it foams. Sir in the boiling water and pinch of salt.

In a separate bowl, mix the flour, cinnamon, brown sugar and butter into crumbs.

Pour 1/3 of the molasses mixture into the unbaked crust. Sprinkle 1/3 of the crumbs over the molasses mixture and continue alternating layers, finishing with the crumbs on top.

Bake in preheated oven for 30 minutes, or until the crumbs and crust are golden.

About the Author

An award-winning, USA Today and Wall Street Journal bestselling author I hope you'll join me *snooping into life's mysteries with fun, fiction, and food—California style!*

Life is an extravaganza! Figuring out how to hang tough and make the most of the wild ride is the challenge. On my way to Oahu, to join the rock musician and high school drop-out I had married in Tijuana, I was nabbed as a runaway. Eventually, the police let me go, but the rock band broke up.

Our next stop: Disney World, where we "worked for the Mouse" as chefs, courtesy of Walt Disney World University Chef's School. More education landed us in academia at The Ohio State University. For decades, I researched, wrote, and taught about many gloriously nerdy topics.

Retired now, I'm still married to the same, sweet guy and live with him near Palm Springs, California. I write the Jessica Huntington Desert Cities Mystery series set here in the Coachella Valley, the Corsario Cove Cozy Mystery Series set in California's Central Coast, The Georgie Shaw Mystery series set in the OC, The Seaview Cottages Cozy Mystery Series set on the so-called American Riviera, just north of Santa Barbara, and The Calla Lily Mystery series that takes place in California's Wine Country. Won't you join me? Sign up at: desertcitiesmystery.com.

Made in the USA
San Bernardino, CA
05 May 2019